*In the heart of
where time bend
this mystical fable was weaved
to reveal secrets adults take for mere tales.*

By the same author

A Book to Free the Soul

The Pearl that Lies in the Sea

A Story & a Covenant

THE PEARL THAT LIES IN THE SEA

Hymnoneos Books. December 21, 2023.

Copyright © 2023 Yves Cadoux.

All rights reserved. This book or parts thereof may not be reproduced, stored in a retrieval system, or transmitted in any form or by any means except in the case of brief, properly credited quotations in articles or reviews.

The scanning, uploading, and distribution of this publication via the internet without the permission of the publisher is illegal. Please, purchase only authorized electronic editions.

ISBN: 9798872598244

Preamble

The memories of my youth are the quivering colors of a fading dream. My soul in the latter years of my life is no longer rigid but pliable, fluid, and receptive. I have become a Janus-like figure, both an old man looking subjectively to the past, and a child gazing imaginatively at the future on a timeline that isn't linear but revolving. Nonetheless, the story as I remember it should be told, a passing cloud in the ineffable sky.

I

I grew up lonely. Life is a desert, each soul a tenuous oasis. And the roads between individuals are fraught with uncertainty. Not that I couldn't make friends, but behind the face of everyone I met, I was looking for something unattainable. I had a mystical bent, and at the outset the path of the mystic is a solitary one. To be sure, there have been passing love interests that made my solitude more bearable, but the idealistic aura through which I perceived them for a season invariably faded out. Hence perhaps, my passion for timeless works of art and literature because no matter how much they are explicated, they retain a measure of mystery. I would learn in time that I was never entirely alone in my plight. There is an invisible fellowship uniting those who are weighed by the incomprehensible heaviness of the soul that the philosopher Bertrand Russell described as *a terrible pain—a curious wild pain—a searching for something beyond what the world contains, something transfigured and infinite.*

I was not religiously educated, but I was intrigued by religious literature. There was a bible in my father's library that I picked up with the serious intent to read it from cover to cover. However, the more I sank my young mind into its matter, the more horrified I was. Why did the god favor Abel's bloody sacrifice over Cain's gentle offering of grains and fruits? Why would Abraham submit to sacrificing his son? Why did the god harden Pharaoh's heart and then punish him for it? And most damning yet, how could a good god purposefully cause multitudes of infants and innocents to die, not just once but several times? As an adult, I read or heard all the possible combinations of disingenuous argumentation that the apologists for the Abrahamic religions could wring out of their brains in their determination to justify the unjustifiable. Regrettably, days would come when I too bent my reason to accommodate impossible excuses. The truth is that most adults are in denial of what an untutored child could see plainly: The good book reveals to mankind a god who is unreasonable, unfair, petty, jealous, revengeful, violent, obsessed with blood, and worshipped by unstable characters. And I certainly wasn't keen on the plethora of insane rules and nonsensical commandments either. From the Old Testament I switched to the New, but it failed to change my mind. The weird miracles, the inconsistencies, the fixation on sin, the glorification of suffering, and the ravings of Paul were too much for me. Thus began and quickly ended my childhood initial foray into the religion of the book.

The same year I took a shot at self-Christianizing (and missed), I was confronted with evil. A teacher had taken a pronounced dislike to me that manifested in a continual disdain punctuated with regular put downs. I had been humiliated before, at a younger age (what child had not?), but that was by my peers; it was different from the calculated, systematic hatred an adult can direct at a less experienced person. Hatred. Even after half a century, I can name it for what it was without exaggeration. I was helpless to understand what could possibly motivate a grown-up man in his sixties to act so vehemently toward a child. I had even defended the man once when another boy was mocking him, which made the pointed derision on his part more painful to bear. The best efforts of less proficient students were met with praise and words of encouragement; my modest achievements were received with sneers. No occasion was missed to ridicule me in front of my classmates, and I knew not how to respond except by letting the barbs shred my heart. Ridicule in the craft of the skilled satirist can be an effective tool of awareness; in the hands of most people, the same tool only serves to divert their mind away from the void and the terror in the innermost of their being. I know that. To my great shame, there was a time I too caused pain, albeit uncommonly, by mocking others who in some respects were less fortunate than I was, or simply because they were different.

II

Winter came. From my bedroom window, I gazed at the portion of gray sky framed by the four inner faces of our building overlooking the narrow courtyard that once accommodated the eighteenth-century stables. Up there, the endlessly fascinating murmurations of the starlings swooped and swirled like airborne jets of black lava and smoke. In summertime, they would be replaced by a gulp of swallows who kept me entertained with impressive stunts. I could always count on that slice of sky to distract me with its aerial performers, falling rain, passing clouds, peeking sun, and changing light.

I played discs on my turntable, songs by Charles Aznavour that spoke of unrequited love or impossible dreams. I read the poetry of "The Decadents." I tarried in the company of the impressionists and the symbolists, immersing myself in their masterpieces from library artbooks and photo slides. It was all nurturing melancholy, at once dolorous and enjoyable: sadness and comfort in a bundle.

Having determined that the authoritarian god who wallows in the desperation and adulation of mankind was an aberration of the mind, I resolved to seek for solace a banished god, a god who was lonely as I was and would certainly hear in his silent exile the cry of a sole worshiper. When the untutored child whose beliefs are yet to be shaped by the religions of man is drawn to worship, he naturally turns to magic rituals. One evening then, I stole through our apartment while everyone was asleep to fetch the two statuettes of African fertility divinities my father had bought from a peddler in Marseille and now proudly displayed on top of his bookshelf. They were mass-produced fakes but looked authentic enough for my purpose. I fashioned a compact sacred space on my bedroom antique rug and drew apart the large curtains to let my private quadrangle of overcast sky reflect the city light with a pale sulfur glow. I lit two candles and positioned the two fertility gods on each side, male and female, underlying the dual reality of all things in the universe and beyond. I undressed completely because it felt entirely good, and slightly subversive. I crayoned stick figures on a piece of paper that I meant to represent the uncontrollable yearning that wrecked the space in my heart where I had let it settle. Then I prostrated before my idols and invoked the numen I had drawn into them much like the ancients would have done in their domestic magical practices.

The following weekend, the family headed to our rural estate as we almost always did in winter. I enjoyed those weekly getaways because, unlike during the summertime vacation, there weren't too many home improvement projects for which my father required my assistance. That meant I could spend the extra time meandering through the agrarian outdoors. Though in the dead of the cooler season the birds were mostly silent and the trees even more so, the mist and the heavy clouds suited my mood. I walked in the woods until both ends of my path were dematerialized by the fog, and I renewed my allegiance to the rebel god. Lying on a felled trunk thick with moss, I offered my body and soul to him who doesn't stand idle at the end of any path but wanders in the heart of the solitary.

III

Winter was running thin, starved by something indefinably spring-like. While an interior breeze was sweeping the dusty corners of my soul, an obsessive daimon of tidiness removed the clutter to make room for fresh possibilities. And in that space came to dissolve at the end of their long journey ripples of an inexpressible desire surging from a time before my time.

I fed the ducks at the public gardens. I dawdled in the web of galleries at the museum of natural history. I bought posters of artworks by Vasarely to decorate my bedroom. On the way to school, I saluted a pygmy owl that had made its abode of a hole in a plane tree. The vicious attacks of my teacher had not abated, but I knew they too, like winter, would not last forever. It was then that I was visited by a wingless seraph.

I had just left the class from hell and sat on the windowsill momentarily to survey the street below while waiting for the students to clear out of the hallway. I did not care about being late for math class, and I thought of a believable excuse I could use. I forced myself to move eventually and was startled by a small, clear, and firm voice when I walked into the stairwell:

"Beware of the hounds of the lord!"

And then, as if in a reply to my mute surprise, it announced again:

"The *domini canis*... they will sniff you out."

From his perch on the steps just below the platform, a boy was observing me intently like a kitten sizing up its new human foster parent with a mixture of curiosity and bravado. His hair was red, thick and supple, agreeably matched by green-blue eyes that pierced me with an elfin stare. His lips were thin and not favorably disposed toward excessive smiling, but his features were overall soft, delicate, and reassuring. He was dressed smartly in the fashion of the day, sporting a lightweight, dark maroon turtleneck sweater over flared-bottom trousers. Around his waist hung a wide belt, and the motif adorning its oversized buckle especially attracted my attention. It was a stylized shooting star in relief, complete with five branches and a tail. (I remember all the details because I envied his trendy outfit compared to the boring clothes my mother made me wear.)

I was never one to know how to make a smooth first introduction. The boy seemed harmless enough, even smaller than I was, and I stepped up to meet him. I wanted to ask what he meant to tell me, but I was still at a loss for words. Making every effort to look nonchalant, I went to lean against the handrail and found myself standing over my unusual interlocutor. On his knees rested a school satchel he used as a surface to support a sketchbook. With masterly skill he was drawing a curious image: two dogs before a pool howling at a crescent-bearing lunar disk rising between two towers. The sprouting artist was gnawing at the tip of his pencil. He looked up and told me:

"Your teacher... he hates you because he knows what you are. He is one of them, the dogs who sleep in the manger of the oxen: they do not eat, and they do not allow the oxen to eat either. But when the dog is gone, what will the ox do?"

I was perplexed and trying to think of something casually clever I could say to make myself worthy of his interest. I was about to congratulate him on his excellent sketching technique when I heard my last name called sharply from higher up the stairs. The school principal was coming down, intent on finding out why I was still loitering in the stairwell after the bell. I was saved by the suitable excuse I had concocted earlier, but I was also briefly distracted away from my diminutive seraphic visitor. When I turned around, he had vanished.

Unlike adults, children are unfazed by the preternatural; they welcome it in their imaginative reality. Thus I wasn't terribly astonished at the main event of the day, and my life resumed its predictable ordinariness. Yet, I couldn't stop mulling over what the unimposing oracle had sought to make me understand and how the principal had apparently failed to notice him. Most of all, I wondered why the boy would vanish so suddenly when, presumably, he intended to befriend me. Or was it I who desperately wanted to believe a *compagnon de voyage* could so easily appear on the shore of my solitude?

IV

Summer came, and my strange visitor had not reentered the dull flow of the days. My disappointment at the missed opportunity and the puzzling questions that lingered afterward were in part tempered by my excitement at a promised trip to Corsica, courtesy of my parents' friends who lived in Bastia. They were decent people, congenial enough, and certainly more carefree and fun to be with than my own family. We took the train and the ferry, which was more thrilling to me than the plane. The boat crossed the Mediterranée over the night, and I spent a good part of it on deck from where I observed a resplendent phenomenon I had never witnessed before. A crimson moon emerged full from the waves, glazing the sea with a trail of blood, and I took it as a fabulous presage. At daybreak, a pod of striped dolphins followed us, leaping above the pacified waters.

V

In many respects, the life of my hosts gave the impression of being an endless vacation, quite removed from the petit bourgeois preoccupations of my kin. They had planned several activities with me in mind, and on a scorching day, they took me to a secluded location in the mountain, a picturesque natural hideaway known only to the local villagers (like nearly all Corsicans living in the main coastal cities, my hosts had relatives in one of the numerous tiny villages that pepper the mountainous landscape). We were joined by still more friends and extended family for what turned out to be one of those Mediterranean outings with plenty of food, interminably animated conversations, Pétanque games, and too much drinking that would extend late into the evening hours. I asked for permission to go explore the environs on my own, and it was granted offhandedly.

The ground cover of fragrant, dry pine needles crackled softly under my feet as I headed toward the warm, white sand of the creek and the swimming holes framed by humongous boulders on the edge of the forested narrow plateau. I jumped into the cooling water and wadded the shallow current, here chasing a trout that darted by, there pursuing a red dragonfly. At a bend, the waters gathered in a deeper, calmer funnel-like pool, and on the opposite bank, perched on a six-foot-tall rock, sat a young fellow with his feet dangling into the void. He had long, red hair coursing down the length of his neck.

I swam across the pool, my expectations high and my heart pounding uncontrollably, determined not to repeat my past miscalculation. Better say something witless than not saying anything at all I decided. Certainly, boys do not need to talk much when they first meet. They size each other up—friend, foe, or indifferent—and that quick determination sets the tone of what happens next. Adults ask all sorts of ludicrous questions, and all the while you never know what they think of you.

I reached the face of the rock and floated on my back below my would-be interlocutor's feet. Pushing against the boulder with my own feet, I propelled myself slightly farther to catch his gaze and initiate the conversation.

"Are you lost?" I asked somewhat awkwardly. It was the best I could manage, and I instantly regretted the silliness of the question. But the lad responded to my genuine effort and saved me the embarrassment by reciprocating.

"I'm looking for a stone," he simply said, which was baffling enough to discourage further lack of originality. But I would not give up; I told him my name and asked for his.

"I am Aristakes," he replied.

I thought that to be positively one of the loveliest names I'd heard, and I felt encouraged by his overture.

"Would you care for a swim, Aristakes?"

"I'm afraid I can't swim."

"I can show you how," I now said confidently.

Aristakes scrambled down his lofty station to join me on the sandy bank where we sat side by side, our butts in the water. With the sun shining on his face, I could see specks of gold in his ethereal green-blue eyes. There was no doubt in my mind, my otherworldly visitant was back, now as a new friend. We spent nearly an hour romping in the creek without much substantial talking. I suspected Aristakes was a bit disingenuous when he said he couldn't swim, for he appeared instantly proficient in the techniques that I clumsily attempted to teach him. All the same, he was quite keen on being affectionate, and I liked the closeness of his lithe body more developed than mine. Indeed, although it had been only a few months since our first, peculiar encounter at school, Aristakes had aged by two to three years while I, evidently, had stayed the same. I recalled his skin to be very fair, almost alabastrine, but now it was tan like the dry needles carpeting the pine grove as if he had been born out of the Corsican soil. Once we had exhausted ourselves in plays, we lounged and basked in the sunshine. That is when I paid more attention to a quaint birthmark I had spied earlier on his abdomen, just below the belly button. It stained his epidermis like dark wine, and I traced its contours with the tip of my finger. The mark had the shape of a star pointing downward.

"It's mid-afternoon already," interrupted Aristakes, "and I still want to show you something no one has seen in a very long time." He stood up.

"Come!" He took my hand gently, and we set off upstream, hopping from boulder to boulder toward the crags until we met the steeper face of the mountain.

"Hop onto my back," my guide said assuredly. I had not realized how light I had become to him. I wrapped my arms around his neck, clasped his waist with my legs, and we began our ascent. He negotiated the crags and cliffs with the assurance and agility of the *muvrone*. I lost perception of time; we were bouncing through it. The sun descended behind the mountain; the upper sky turned aquamarine and the rock ocher. Wide beams of light like golden gossamer interspersed with the long shadows that had acquired a bluish tinge. We covered the last stretch to our destination by climbing steps that had been naturally eroded out of the rock. They led us to a large hollow in the peak that preceded a narrower tunnel like a chthonic respiratory tract. Perhaps wild animals still used the grotto as a shelter from the elements, but unfamiliar markings on its walls suggested that ancient visitors much like us were once here for their own purpose. We sat in the mouth of the cave where we could feel its cool breath. Facing the sea in the east, we listened to the song of the night when everything that seemed dead during the day seemingly comes to life in the dark. Silence between the two of us wasn't an awkward companion and would become a reliable friend.

"Do you want to hear a story?" asked Aristakes after a while.

"Mm-hmm."

"There was once on this island a donkey driver called Andria. The youth had lost his father to a vendetta at a young age. He knew firsthand the brutality of men. His mother, Petra, raised him jealously. He had taken up the family trade, transporting people and goods for merchants and travelers, soldiers and smugglers. Because of his reliability, knowledge of routes and terrains, and evident foreknowledge of the whereabouts of bandits, his services were in demand and well paid. One late autumn evening, Andria was crossing a chestnut grove on his way back home. Only the swishing sound of the soaked dead leaves trampled under the hooves of the donkeys could be heard against the exquisitely absolute silence. Even without the sun, the yellow, ocher, and golden shades of the foliage everywhere tinted the atmosphere with a spellbinding luminosity. It was a stage fit for the entrance of a fairytale personage or a mythic creature, but instead, it was another youth whom Andria spotted at a distance. With one hand on the grip of his pistol, the donkey driver opted for a cautious approach. But as he drew nearer, he decided the stranger was harmless enough, unarmed as he was, and rather despondent looking, seated between the roots of the largest tree, his knees drawn under his chin and his shins grasped in his arms.

'Hello! Are you lost?'

The adolescent looked up. His hair was the color of the ripe chestnut, his eyes were amber, and when they met Andria's gaze, the donkey driver was smitten by the regal, ephebic beauty of the stranger who looked like a prince in exile, a sovereign without a kingdom, alone among the trees of an enchanted forest.

'What is your name?' inquired Andria.

'Lisandru.'

'Are you lost, Lisandru?' repeated Andria. 'What are you doing in these parts?'

'I was looking for the stone that will set me free, and I heard you coming from afar.'

The answer did not satisfy the donkey driver, but he was already bound by the spell the enigmatic traveler had cast on him.

'Are you cold? Hungry? Will you come to my house? And I will care for your needs.'

And Lisandru followed Andria. And six seasons passed."

Aristakes suspended the momentum of his story.

"Do you know what 'Lisandru' means?"

"Unh-uh."

"It means 'Protector of mankind.' Same as "Alexander," which was the name of a great conqueror. Alexander had a friend called Hephaestion. When Hephaestion died, Alexander was devastated, reportedly refusing to eat and sleep for days."

I knew about Alexander from history lessons, but I did not want to interrupt Aristakes' observations. He fascinated me, and all I cared about was being the center of his attention. I relished seeing how evidently delighted he was in sharing his knowledge with me.

"Alexander loved and guarded Hephaestion like the pupil of his eye because when he looked at his faithful friend, he could see the reflection of his very own soul. And Lisandru too loved Andria. But Andria's mother took a profound dislike of Lisandru from the start, fearing that he would take her child from her. She complained to her son that his companion did nothing but compose verses by night and by day roam the woods and gulches, looking for God knows what. In truth, Lisandru wasn't useless. He taught Andria how to read, write, and the fundamentals of arithmetic, which considerably helped in expanding the donkey driver's family business. Lisandru also had a knowledge of plants, salves, and potions and cured many elderlies of their ills and pains. He showed the children of the villagers how to tame wild beasts and whisper charms to have the birds carry messages to distant places. But Petra told her son that Lisandru could not be trusted, and Andria always deferred to his mother.

One summer evening, on their way back from bathing in the pools of the mountain creek, as they often did, the two youths took a shortcut through the chestnut grove where they had first met. In the stillness guarded by the venerable trees, Lisandru spoke first:

'All you see is a veiled weaved before your eyes by the artificers of faith, hope, and morality. I come from a place that lies beyond; I wish to take you there. And though your mind is in chains, I will free your soul.'

Andria couldn't make much sense of what his companion was telling him, and so Lisandru clarified:

'Come with me to my kingdom, and you will never grow old. I will repay your kindness to me a hundred-fold, and we will be together forever.'

Andria was torn. He wanted to be with Lisandru, but he wouldn't go against the wishes of his mother. He wanted to be loved, but he craved recognition among his people even more. He also thought his friend to be a sorcerer more than he believed his claim to be the potentate of a distant, improbable kingdom.

'If you choose this world over mine, all will be lost,' said Lisandru. 'Very soon you will have so many memories, you will forget what is essential.'

Lisandru indeed did not show any sign of aging while Andria was fast becoming a man, and the prospect suited him. He'd had enough with poetry and this nonsense about eternal youth. The enchantment of Lisandru's chimeras was wearing off, and the world of men was calling him.

'You were searching for a treasure,' Andria retorted at last. 'Perhaps you should go on with your quest. I will always be here for you when you decide to return.'

The moment he had spoken the words, he already regretted them. Words are spells; once they have been released, and even if retracted, it is fiendishly difficult to prevent them from carrying their intent. Andria looked into Lisandru's amber eyes, and he wished time would stop and reverse its course. But nothing of the sort happened. He reached with his hand for the ever-youthful face, but instead, it was the antler of a red deer that his fingers brushed. The animal cast a last, mournful glance at Andria and galloped away into the rising shadows at the edge of the grove.

As soon as he had returned to his house, Andria tried to forget. In time, he married, and his business prospered. Petra constantly reminded him he had done right. Indeed, he had become mayor of his village, and an influential man too. Alas, he grew old. And then, visitors to these parts often reported seeing in the forest a lone figure weeping before the exposed roots of a large tree."

Promising myself that I would not repeat Andria's misjudgment, I told the storyteller:

"I will never leave you." And calmly he responded:

"No man can serve two masters, or else he would be devoted to one and the other he would despise. While in the dark, you scurry about like a measly creature of the dark. When the light of dawn shines on you, what will you do?"

On the epidermis of his neck, I smelled the entrancing fragrances of cypress and geranium, searing sands and salty winds, as if the pores could retain the olfactory memory of all the places he had visited. I surrendered to the mellow embrace of a nocturnal kinship and was transported into a pleasant distortion of reality. A lunar disk accented with a thin and brilliant crescent hung above me like a locket pinned on the skin of the night. I reached with my fingers to unlock its inner mystery, and pearls of moonshine dripped on my body, mixing and slithering with droplets of perspiration. Out of a languid rapture, I asked softly:

"How will I see you again?" And exhaled from the lung of the cave I heard an answer like a murmur:

"Follow the firefly."

I woke up lying supine on the back seat of the car. Staring at the starry vault, I thought that the milky way cut through the rear window like the band of freckles on Aristakes' face. I could hear the day trippers exchanging goodnight wishes before destination was a small church that stuck out amidst the cultivated land and had for the longest time excited my curiosity from afar. Now my interest was renewed because I was certain the religious edifice stood in the very direction the firefly had taken before I lost sight of it.

Up close, the structure was a letdown: plain, derelict, and boarded up. I stood awhile planted on the dirt path, unable to decide what to do next. But I heard, wafting from the neighboring cluster of trees, the faint sound of dribbling water, like a pleasant invitation. And when I penetrated the shade of the canopy, I discovered nested in a clearing of brambles and nettles, a rustic fountain on the ledge of which sat Aristakes waiting. He looked like he was expecting me and showed no surprise, impassive as ever. I, on the other hand, ran and threw myself in his arms. He was elegantly attired all in white as if for a religious occasion, with a polo shirt tucked in fitted shorts, cool Converse shoes, and immaculate socks; I was shirtless, with dirty shorts and flip-flops.

"Let's go to the church; I wanna see what's inside," I told him excitedly. He followed somewhat reluctantly, but at the same time eager to please me. We split and looked for a way in, but all the windows were solidly shuttered, and the door barricaded. I was about to give up when a loud crack suggested a breach. Retracing my steps back to the main entrance, I found my prince beaming from the inside, in front of a heap of shattered planks and the remnants of what certainly had been the door.

The interior was as disappointing as the exterior; there was nothing in there except noxious mold, cobwebs, and dusty debris.

"This place reeks of shame and desperation," complained Aristakes. "Do you know why the ancients sought to make their temples, churches, or mosques so elaborate and ornate?"

I did not need answering to have him pursue:

"...Because they thought an otherworldly aesthetic would somehow palliate the toxic tide that flows in through the gates with the faithful. Houses of worship nowadays are either bland or gaudy, and without the tempering effect of beauty and harmony, their atmosphere is saturated with the worshippers' pain, guilt, false hopes, sordid confessions, and hypocrisy."

That put the final damper on my curiosity. We gladly walked out of the building and into the brightness of the season. The scenery about us spread like a canvas painted by Camille Corot: cultivated fields, spinneys, meadows, and a sleepy hilltop village on the horizon. We went back to the fountain, Aristakes pulling ahead of me. With poise and grace, he removed his clothes and stepped into the basin where he beckoned me. I tossed what little I had on and joined him. And his words to me were soothing lyrics set to the music of the trickling water:

"When you were one, you became two. But if you have become two, what will you do?"

He was exceedingly fond of riddles. And when I wasn't under their spell, I dismissed them indulgently on account of my friend's enthusiasm for stagey dramatics. But in my latter years, they would come back to haunt me.

That day, I drank from the spout of the fount, and I became intoxicated with its bubbling water, wishing those summer days would last forever.

Early in the evening I returned home for supper, but before we parted, Aristakes enjoined me to meet him on the road that same night.

"I will show you a real temple the likes of which you have never seen," he promised. Nothing more needed to be said to convince me.

I went to bed early and slept for a couple of hours. When the house had fallen entirely silent but for the galloping of country mice between the ceiling of my room and the attic's floor, I decamped through the window, climbing down the vine that creeped on the outside walls. At once, I was bewitched and tranquilized by the luscious scents that passing showers and lower temperatures unlock through the alchemy of the night—a mixed aroma of the vegetal and mineral kingdoms, unknown to the day. The silvery glow of a gibbous moon lit the unclouded sky. The road cut through the cropland with the sheen of a Tahitian pearl. Aristakes was easy to find. I had packed snacks; he had brought two hurricane lanterns. We walked just under two kilometers to a neighboring farm. I knew the farmer because my family bought fresh milk from him that I transported on my bike in a big aluminum can. I had also heard the rumors of a Roman equestrian mosaic he had dissimulated under a pile of manure because he was afraid officials would come digging holes on his property. My father had told me that there was also an antiquated tunnel the farmer was too scared to explore.

The farm was noiseless except for the occasional mooing of a cow. We passed the old dog who I feared would give us away, but the animal kept quiet after Aristakes patted him gently on the head. We went straight to the stone barn where the straw bales were stored. Under Aristakes' precise direction, we moved a few bundles to uncover a clever passageway through which we had to crawl before reaching a chamber at the center of the stack. It was all very impressive to me.

"The farmer's son made that without anyone knowing it," informed Aristakes. "Like that, he and his special friend could meet in secret. Little did he know what bigger secrets lie deeper."

We racked straw off the beaten earth and dug a few centimeters of dirt with Aristakes' pocketknife and a piece of wood until we exposed rotting planks that had been placed over a hole in the ground. A shaft had been unevenly filled in haste with debris to obstruct the passage of an adult, but there was still enough space for a small-framed child to slither through once a few stones and bricks were removed. Down we went. Aristakes helped me, unraveling the same unusually developed panoply of skills to navigate the underground that he had displayed when negotiating the heights of the mountains. We landed into a stepped corridor that led us to an empty vestibule adjoining a large, cavernous area. There, I was petrified in awe.

"This is the holy sanctuary of Mithras," announced Aristakes with a flair for theatrics. "The syncretic god to end all the gods, the eternal father, epitome of all the divinities from Zeus to Christ. His worship hails from time immemorial. He was the first god of friendship, and the Manichaeans regarded him as the living spirit, the soul's angel of liberation who rescues her from demonic darkness. In his court seat Sol and Luna, Hermes and Serapis, Eros and Psyche, the four seasons and the Twelve Signs. And his followers were generously granted salvation and immortality." Aristakes gave me time to scan the place and walk through, to appreciate each part and corner as they were revealed in the light of our lanterns. Still, in the dimness, it was difficult to tell what part of the excavation was man-made and which owed its shape to underground erosion. My companion followed close behind but offered no comment or explanation.

The elongated structure's central aisle was flanked by rows of facing stone benches that lined its two opposite walls. At the farthest end of the grotto was an altar topped with a double-sided, painted high relief. The layout looked to me like the inside of a church of which only the choir and apse would remain. Behind the altar, a flume made of stones channeled a subterranean stream whose water, Aristakes indicated to me, alimented the very fountain in which we had bathed the day before. On the back wall of the "apse," a narrow niche above the flume featured a diminutive statue of the youthful Mithras born out of a rock. The initiands would have starred at the face of the relief that represented Mithras killing the bull. The other side facing the stream showed a naked Helios crowned with a diadem of seven rays and leaning over his companion Mithras. The mystical friends lay on a couch with a light meal of grapes and rolls before them. On each side of the altar was positioned the statuette of a young torchbearer (they are called Cautes and Cautopates). To the left, the boy figurine held a burning torch pointed down. To the right, his twin carried the torch pointing upwards. They stood undisturbed in the same spot where they had been left so long ago as if we were the first visitors to the Mithraeum since it had shut down. But we were not.

Adjacent to the great hall was an exiguous circular room that appeared to have been fashioned haphazardly and in haste. Unlike the rest of the temple, it was unadorned and bare but for the three rough sarcophagi dug in the ground and overlaid with slates. Their slab stone covers had been dragged to the side. Two of them contained scattered skeletal remains, but the third in the middle was empty.

We left the crypt and went to sit cross-legged on the floor of the central aisle. The flickers of the flames in our lanterns animated the bright frescoes on the wall, and their intriguing allegorical figures and mysterious symbols seemingly came to life. The vaulted ceiling was painted blue with golden stars. We lowered the output on the lamps to save fuel.

"Now I can tell you about the stone," said Aristakes. He tucked a bang of hair behind his ear (it never stayed there for long), signaling he was ready to start his story. And I lent an attentive ear to the tale narrated in a low voice with the attention the votary must have once given to the pater who instructed him in the degree of his initiation.

"The story begins before any story was recorded, when mankind had yet to walk the earth, and Gods and Titans fought over who would dominate the cosmos. Zeus, the king of the gods, had an affair with Persephone, the wife of Hades, King of the underworld. The queen gave birth to Zeus' illegitimate son whom they called Dionysus. And the happy father asked Hephaestus, God of the blacksmiths and metalworkers, to craft a weightless golden diadem for the infant. Zeus then took the last starlight that shined in the sky just before dawn and put it in a stone he lodged on the diadem. Hera was the legitimate wife of Zeus, and in a fit of jealousy she resolved to have the young Dionysus murdered. She incited the Titans to slay the child while he was distracted playing with the stone of the diadem. The Titans attacked Dionysus, dismembered him, and devoured the parts. When Zeus found out, in a rage he destroyed the Titans with thunderbolts. After the smoke and vapors had lifted from the scene of the carnage, all that remained of the Titans was ashes and blood on the ground. But amidst the splatter lay popes. When the 27th canon of the Third Council of Lateran was promulgated by the church of Rome, she was proclaimed a heretic herself. The Lady de Caraman's domain was pillaged, her friends were tortured and condemned to an ignominious death that she barely escaped by flying into exile.

"It's getting late," submitted Aristakes putting a halt to his story.

"Your stories are always sad," I commented, to which he responded:

"Whosoever has known the world has stumbled upon a decaying corpse, and whosoever has stumbled upon that corpse, of him the world is not worthy."

I would never have remembered his enigmatic sayings hadn't I found many years later that they were inspired by or cited from apocryphal sources. As usual, he continued notwithstanding my bewildered gaze.

"People like to hear happy stories to make themselves feel good because of the sadness of the world. But when they truly want to learn about themselves or the nature of the world, they will listen to sad stories."

I gave him one of my sandwiches, which he declined because of the meat he wouldn't eat. But the offerings of my fruits he took gladly. And on that happy night, in darkness and concealment, seen of none, Aristakes began to instruct me in the degrees of his own mysteries.

VII

Following our visit to the Mithraeum, I slept late, lazed about, and indulged in sentimental fantasies about being admitted at the ancient princely court of a luminous kingdom far removed from this existence, earth, and the cosmos. Aristakes had asked me to meet him two days hence at the ruins of the watermill, by the river. I knew the location precisely because my father used to take me fishing in the proximity. (That was before I swore off fishing subsequent to a wrenching burst of compassion when I clumsily gutted a fish alive trying to remove the hook it had swallowed.) Anglers are notoriously secretive about their favorite spots, and so the place was rarely visited. The waterline had long receded from where the mill was originally built, and its ruins now stood in a clearing amidst the alders, ashes, and willows. There wasn't much left of the old structure but scattered rubble and an oversized millstone, curiously propped by debris like an altar to the resident spirits. It had been left alone for centuries, perhaps on account of the rumors it was once the epicenter of esoteric, pagan rituals.

My companion and I selected a spot to make ourselves comfortable. This time I had brought vegetarian sandwiches only. If my friend abstained from meat, it was good enough for me as well. The songs of the woodland birds pierced the uninterrupted white noise of the river flow, and the raconteur transported us against the course of time to the conclusion of his story. His tone, however, was no longer that of a distanced narrator but had the vibrancy of a personal account, as if he had witnessed the very events he described.

"In a late afternoon of summer 1182, Aurèlia de Caraman was standing on the jutting boulder that overlooked a crystalline pool high in the insular mountains of her exile. The place was once sacred to ancient dwellers of the island, but the Lady's business there was the opposite of worship. Far from seeking an ecstatic communion with the numen of the creek, she was intent on extracting herself from the exacting passion the object in her hand exerted on her whole person. Yet, the moment she was to break the spell, she was overwhelmed by dolefulness and regret like one who ought to part with her lover, knowing that fate is irreversibly pulling them in different directions. The stone nested in her cupped hand felt cool on the palm. It always had that feel to the touch, a curiously comforting coolness. The gem was uncut, unshaped by a man's tools, but smoothed and polished by its owners' touch through generations. One remarkable feature was its translucent, vivid blue that gave the impression of veiling an inner light and acquired a tinge of green when layering the moon but sparks of amber when filtering the sunrays. And it had another secret too: if you put it close to your ear at dawn or at dusk, you could hear it sing a lament in a strange language. Many times, Aurèlia had done so until she convinced herself she could understand the words:

To free the radiant pearl, the true heir is come from afar; the pearl that lay deep in the sea, the fallen star.

Aurèlia had been warned in a dream to release her possession to its destiny, that it wasn't hers to keep. Furthermore, a powerful entity and its cohorts were after the stone, she learned, which would only compound her woes. The Lady was too familiar with omens and portents to ignore the foreboding. She gazed at the stone longingly one last time and dropped it. The treasured gift plummeted erratically to the white bed of the creek, and its contrasting blue shape quivered in the current before the bitsy grains of sand rolled over their bigger kin greedily, swallowing it in the grasp of their multitude."

"Do you think we can find the stone?" I interjected enthusiastically.

"The stone is like a farmer who has a treasure hidden in his field and does not know it."

Obviously... The moment I had inquired, I knew the answer to my question wouldn't be what I wanted to hear, but I did not mind anymore. I knew Aristakes was working through me. I was on his side. I had to be patient and learn. He was the sower; I was his field. But the ground had to be tilled first. And on that day, on the altar amidst the alders, we took the sacrament of Aristakes' religion, which he called the religion of knowledge and beauty.

"I have a present for you," said my hierophant. And in my hand, he placed a polished amber stone with a firefly trapped in it.

"Fireflies are shy; they do not go to cities. But this one will accompany you everywhere. And when it glows, you will know I am calling you. This light will guide you more surely than the noonday sun to the place where I'll be waiting for you. Look then for the closest library or museum about you; that is where you'll find me." And I understood that my companion, like the swifts, would go away at summer's end.

VIII

I went back to school, advancing to the next grade and getting rid of my tormentor in the process. But an education provided by the state now looked frivolous compared to what I had to gain by following Aristakes wherever he might lead me. Where he was and when he would summon me though, I did not know. So, life in most respects resumed what we call normalcy, and I again fell into a gloom.

Fortunately, a crisp afternoon in late autumn would break at last the weighty trance of familiarity. I was taking an aimless stroll through the streets of the city when the amber piece (which I had taken to wearing around my neck with a string) started to glow at the junction of Rue d'Alsace and Rue de Metz. I was standing across the street from the Musée des Augustins. Remembering Aristakes' promise, I all but ran to the ticket office window and purchased a student admission ticket. I proceeded to systematically walk through all the galleries at a steady pace until I found my friend focused on examining a rather unremarkable rendition of *Saint Michael's Slaying of the Rebel Angels* by an eighteenth-century local painter. The solemnity of the place did not lend itself to exuberant displays of affection, and Aristakes was into his customary stoic act, so I just sat quietly beside him waiting for the silence to be broken.

"Do you know what the name Michael means?" I did not, but it did not matter. By then, I expected his questions never to concern themselves with my answer. I did not utter a sound, and sure enough he carried on.

"It comes from the Hebrew and means 'who is like God.' Isn't that odd then: The painting represents *who is like God* striving to thwart the ascent of *who will be like the Most High*." He gave me a minute to ponder the information and hopped to another train of thought.

"Let's go somewhere else. This painter is no Raphael, and his piece is awfully depressing." I agreed.

He must have had the location in mind for he walked uninterruptedly at a brisk pace, with me in tow, until he stopped unhesitatingly before Laurent-Honoré Marqueste's dynamic *Cupidon*.

"That is much, much better," announced my impromptu tour guide before launching into his next monologue.

"Nietzsche wrote that without ecstasy, no art would be possible. But ecstasy rises from the flame of desire, and there is no purer desire than that which is born on the ashes of despair. Despair, desire, and ecstasy are the unrivaled producers of the loftiest expressions of art.

"You know, museums are a very recent phenomenon. Art was never meant to be hoarded in one place for people to come and see; it was once part of their lives and all around them, in streets, public squares, official buildings, places of worship, and private homes. They understood then, as Aldous Huxley submitted, that *art is a protest against the horrible inclemency of life*."

After noting the many forms of Desire for a while, we moved along and went sitting between the columns of the cloister, facing the garth. Aristakes had more to say.

"It isn't surprising this monastery was turned into a museum of fine arts; both are sanctuaries. Look at the people who come here, they no longer appear so frantic: They murmur, take their time, and fall into moments of contemplation as if they were in a church. Yet, at church, the faithful expect to be filled with something but never quite manage to leave at the door the baggage they carry throughout their existence. At a museum or a library, the patrons empty themselves before stepping in so that they can be filled with beauty and knowledge. The Arts have never fostered violence, greed, and narrow-mindedness but religions have and continue to do so. And the world of adults is afraid of uncensored knowledge. When children hear that Santa Claus is a myth, they do not attempt to deny it. They are upset for a few minutes and then eager to share the scoop with their friends. When the fallacy of their myths is demonstrated to adults, they deny it. Then they become terribly upset and go to great lengths to shield themselves from doubt. Only adults are afraid to hear or read what they do not want to be true. Children want to learn everything and are afraid of very little. And yet, it is the adult who decides what the child should or shouldn't hear and read. What is the logic behind this system? It is the logic of control. Knowledge everywhere in the world is regulated. The purveyors of information decide what must and must not reach you between the cradle and the grave. Paradoxically, you become one of them too when you grow up. They have taken the keys of gnosis and hid them. They do not enter the temple of Wisdom, and those who desire to enter they will not let in. But you yourself must become wise like the serpent and remain innocent like a dove."

The following weeks, my friend took me on a grand tour of the forbidden and the heretical, and I bit that apple ravenously. I filled a notebook with his recommendations of books and films. In fact, 50 years later, I have the list with me still, and it has a few remaining items yet to be checked. And I laugh at the fatuity of the world who would never learn that simple lesson: The more you want to hide something from the child, the more it will excite his curiosity.

This was the longest I had been with Aristakes, and it made me feel invulnerable. I believed there was a future that belonged to the both of us, that we would never be without each other. One day, he unexpectedly embraced me in a tight hug without saying a word. And it was like blasting a wall to reveal a hitherto unknown horizon. Free of earthly gravity, I soared like a swift above the seas and the mountain peaks, and I felt in my being the apotheosis of Ganymede.

Aristakes left me once again, but I had more than the promise of his return; I had the elation of surrender, when passion is more precious than choice.

IX

School was less of a burden. Not that I was doing well—quite the contrary—but I had no longer a personal stake in being chiseled like a tiny gear for the monstrous machinery of the world. I began living a double life: one for the mundane reality, one in a transmundane reality of my own. As a result, my report card too had become a sad reality in itself. Among the offenders who lined up before my aggrieved parents, the worst was my performance in German language. To remedy the deficiency, they opted to send me to a summer academic program: three weeks of intensive German language immersion. Germany itself was out of budget, but Alsace, the alternative across the border, was just right. The summer camp solution also came with a silver lining. At the end of the study program, I was to spend the remainder of my vacation time in Paris with my mom's childhood friend and her son. Things weren't going well between my parents and keeping me away for a while would benefit everyone.

Despite the unfortunate implications the academic disaster would have for my later years, I have no regrets. I still consider the only life worth living to be that of the imagination. After all, it is where human beings spend the greatest share of their time whether they realize it or not. That is also the only place where we are relatively free from the chains of cause and effect and from an existence scripted by consequences. Children naturally understand the rules and advantages of imagination, and that is why, among many other things, childhood is more valuable than adulthood. Aristakes once told me that eternal youth can be compared to a fisherman's son who finds a priceless pearl in his father's harvest and keeps it for himself. He also said that not just the children, but the adults too give credence to tall tales—perhaps even more so. "The difference," he clarified "is that the former knowingly invent the stories they want to believe whereas the latter believe the stories others make up for them."

Imagination is the seat of those fanciful memories we believe are actual, the source of absurd religious myths we take for facts, and the only place where romantic love perdures, though we try to convince ourselves otherwise. Imagination then is the parallel life that makes existence bearable for most of us. Hence, I am not dwelling on the parts of my existence from which Aristakes was absent, because he was the nexus of my imaginative potentialities.

X

For Christmas I received from my uncle a book that I would cherish for many years until I deemed it too childish to keep. It was a superbly illustrated collection of captivating Scandinavian tales, and two of them in particular reminded me of my involvement and adventures with Aristakes.

The first told the story of Olaf, the young son of the Lord of Flagh-Staad. Olaf liked to take long walks by the sea and rescued helpless animals. One day, he saves a colony of seagulls from the attack of a vicious raptor. He is then led to an enchanted grotto and meets the king of the elves who gives him a precious stone as a reward for his selflessness and bravery. And Olaf hides the stone in the garden of his father's castle because he is under an oath never to reveal the existence of the elves.

The other story was that of Nadod, an Icelandic shepherd boy who wanted to fly. One day,

Nadod meets a young stranger who, as a thank you for the boy's generous hospitality, offers to put him on a path to make his wish come true. The traveler takes the shepherd on his horse who soars through the clouds and above the sea. And thus, before advancing on the perilous journey to fulfill his dream, Nadod discovers that his mysterious benefactor is no less than the god Thor, Protector of mankind.

The tales got me thinking about the stone of Dionysus and my own benefactor. Why was Aristakes seeking the gem? Why did it exert such fascination on him? What was its secret, its power? The riddles filled me with thrilling curiosity, and I researched as much as I could about the myths and lore of stones throughout history and cultures. Perhaps if I could help him find the stone, my companion would never leave me again. I wanted him to need me as much as I needed him.

The swifts at last returned from their lengthy journey to Africa, and I set my expectation on the approaching return of the summer vacations. At the end of the school year, I was already packed up. No student had ever been so eager to spend the first weeks of summer in a study program. I had an ulterior motive of course. Once again, I traveled by train, which I always enjoyed, and alone this time, which was a bonus. I felt unhindered. At the Strasbourg station, on the other hand, I was greeted by a program instructor, and it dawned on me that I was going to be kept on a short leash.

We were always in supervised groups for everything we did short of bathroom breaks. The Monday-to-Saturday four-hour morning class was a bore despite its being advertised in the brochure as "interactive fun." I made a half-hearted effort because my parents had invested their hopes and money in this last-ditch attempt at my scholastic redemption. Try as I might though, I could never reconcile my vagabond spirit with the Teutonic rigors. I forced myself to focus, but my mind kept escaping through the window to join the swallows in their aerial acrobatics. In fairness, there were also some good moments. We had many activities designed to be recreational, including touring the city. I made a couple of roguish friends who provided a welcome relief to my growing apprehension that Aristakes might not show up.

The last Saturday before our expected Sunday farewell was saved for a taste of German food at the restaurant and a visit to the cathedral Notre Dame de Strasbourg. The plan was to make the ascent to the towers' viewing platform and then to tour the rest of the edifice. At last, I saw the opportunity for a break. I told our chaperons that I had a heart murmur (something I had seen on TV), and that I didn't have the constitution to climb the 330 steps to the top. It worked. With two dozen rowdy children at 66 meters altitude, none of the only two instructors (miraculously, the third had called in sick) could be spared to stay behind with me. A decision then was made for me to wait inside the cathedral for the return of our party, the consensus being that a religious sanctuary was a safe place to leave a minor unsupervised for a couple of hours. I watched as a single file of children was being swallowed in the throat of the tower like the offspring of Cronus devoured by their father, and I went looking for a seat in the nave where I would not be bothered by anyone. Feeling vaguely dejected, I regretted not going to the platform, but I also wanted to be alone. Tourists crowded the cathedral. A group of boarding school students in uniform were scattered around sketching elements of the interior. Their summer camp looked more fun than mine. Hands in my pockets, I dragged my feet along the side aisles to admire the stained-glass windows, slowly making my way toward the choir. I wished I had been there for the equinox, when the famed "rayon vert" would materialize. But perhaps I could ferret out an unsung substitute marvel if I searched hard enough.

    I noticed one of the students sitting on the far eastern end of the nave by himself, apart from the others, like a stray lamb. I approached soundlessly from behind until I could steal a peek at his drawing, and it was nothing I expected. The boy had drawn the tower of the cathedral seemingly on fire with its spire tumbling down. My astonishment was short-lived, quickly giving way to confusion and hesitation because the fine artist in short trousers turned around and fixed me with confident clear gray eyes. His unique smile was unmistakable though:

Aristakes once more playing with morphological disguise. I couldn't tell then which of his appearances was authentically him (they all were), but he was always betrayed by one of these rare smiles, at once haughty and naughty, knowing and teasing, self-assured and playful. The same smile I think one could discern on the lips of Tutankhaten (or at least his wooden semblance, a bust of the young Pharaoh that would end up in his grave), the living image of the sun, the boy who inherited an empire. And again, I found it on the open face of the boy servant Cecco, Caravaggio's model who would become alternatively a saint, an angel, or a god on the painter's canvases. But this was my Aristakes, even though he was at present barely older than the first time he materialized in my life. His hair was now light blonde, shorter, and neatly combed. His lips were fuller, and he had a gap between his front teeth that showed every time he laughed (which he was more frequently inclined to do than before). Once again, the reverent ambience made me hesitant to display too much familiarity, but surprisingly, it was he this time who affectionately wrapped his arms around my waist. There was about him a disconcerting mixture of childishness and ageless maturity, or wisdom. I was now one head taller than him, and I lifted his body off the floor.

"I thought you did not like churches," I said mischievously.

"They are useless," he responded dismissively. "Well... I do have a weakness for the gothic ones: the architectural aesthetics, the structural prowess, the esoteric, whimsical, irreverent, even salacious references left in the stone by the carvers who so annoyed Bernard of Clairvaux. But mainly, it is the stained-glass windows that bring me here.

"Speaking of which," he pursued while motioning with his hand towards the image of Mary transfixed in the colored glass just above the altar, "isn't that curious that she is forced by the priests to stare for ever more at the instrument of torture that killed her son?"

Indeed, on the altar stood erect a large, bare golden cross.

"No matter how you put it, this thing can never be about hope. The inverted cross of Saint Peter represents the unfortunate fall of seraphic essence into matter, with the long vertical axis penetrating the short, horizontal one. The upright cross signifies the striving of that same essence to break free, but the heaviness of matter thwarts its effort. Essence is nailed to the glitter of matter.

"For us though," he continued after a brief silence, "there is a way out.

"C'mon." Aristakes stood and took my hand. "We do not have much time, and there is something I want to show you. Hold my hand tight, and do not let go."

We moved unnaturally, faster than I believed we could, unhampered by any obstacles on the way. I lost my bearings as we pulled through doors and narrow stairwells, and there wasn't a lock that didn't yield to Aristakes' mere touch. We ascended through the innards of the cathedral until we found the attic. Over us loomed countless oakwood beams aligned like immobile, silent sentinels charged to keep something inestimably precious from escaping. At the west end of the loft, the last door unlocked and yawned before Aristakes like a clam shell about to reveal its priceless pearl. I fell on my knees.

Just a few meters away across the dizzying pit floated in the penumbra an immense wheel of translucent colors: the westward rose window I had missed by walking through the nave my back turned to the main portal. It gave the impression of a point of egress into the wonders of a paracosm simultaneously so near and yet unreachable. Its gentle gravity kept the iridescence from radiating too distantly but just enough to beckon you softly, like a siren's charm, to walk across the void and penetrate the soothing, kaleidoscopic light source.

Aristakes broke the spell when I felt his lips brushing my earlobes, and the faint puff of whispers on my skin:

"The ears of grains wedged between the spokes are the Heirs of Dawn who stem from the fertile ground. And the stalks all draw their brightness from the common center that unites them. Thus, the secret of the wheel lies between the five ruby-red glass gems on its hub. Can you see them?"

I could indeed see them, and I expected him to tell me more, but instead, at his unseen command, the door closed slowly, without a noise.

"Remember," he said, "the pilgrims enter through the main portal, but only the heirs leave through the concealed gateway."

And I thought he was referring to the doorways metaphorically, as if speaking in parables.

"Close your eyes," he asked.

"I will be ahead of you in Paris. Meet me at the Louvre. Find the god before whom all knees bend."

There was a sudden draft that caused me to reopen my eyes promptly, but I wasn't in the attic anymore, and neither was Aristakes. I looked about me; my eyesight was slightly blurry. I was sitting in the nave before the choir as if I had never left. Herr T., my German instructor, popped up.

"You missed quite something up-there. Come with us, the tour is about to start. Our guide promised to reveal to us all the secrets of the cathedral." In his enthusiasm, he had forgotten to address me in German.

XI

Violette was a divorced mother and childhood friend of my mother. She and her son Emmanuel, or "Manu" for short, lived in one of those bohemian Parisian mansard apartments, which I thought was the ultimate home. From Manu's bedroom, we could contemplate the immutable gray sea of the zinc roof sheets like the captain of a galleon would have gazed at the ocean waves from the windows of his sterncastle. In lieu of the plaintive cries of the marine birds, the pigeons cooed on the roof slopes, and above them, the swifts sent out their daring calls. Higher up still, the celestial luminaries competed for the best show over the lofty stage while the passing seasons each would leave their signature imprints on the raiment of the sky.

I liked my hosts. She was a great cook and held interesting conversations; he was nice and friendly to me. Manu was supposed to chaperon me for the duration of my stay, but at sixteen, he had far more pressing interests than babysitting. Three days after my arrival, I easily bribed him into cutting me loose. It was a mutually beneficial agreement. Every day, we met at the same hour and metro station before going back home together with the same story. We were each other's alibi, and I did not care what his "crimes" were no matter how he strained to make them sound captivating. I told him mine were to visit bookstores and museums. It was the partial truth he never believed, and he kept pressing me with questions. We could have been solid friends if not for the irresistible pull of my strange life where the eternal love of an improbable being was more desirable than a temporal friendship.

At the first opportunity, I headed to the Louvre Museum. I knew Aristakes would be there regardless of when I showed up, because our time had no hold on him. My passable familiarity with French poetry and art history helped me solve his latter riddle. I knew how fond he was to puzzle me, and I did not mind. His happiness was my happiness. But I would be proud to show him I was able to answer his challenge, though he probably knew that already.

For all our professed devoutness of religious folks, few if any wouldn't abandon their god in a heartbeat for a night of unbridled passion in the arms of a lover (just ask David or Solomon), unless that god was Amor himself. It has been said that Eros is our only master, past, present, and future regardless of who we might be, and none epitomizes his power better than Étienne Maurice Falconet's diminutive *Amour Menaçant*. Thus I found Aristakes respectfully standing before the wee god at the Louvre, and this time around my friend had not changed. He was the same well-mannered, slightly formal boy I had met in Strasbourg, with his neatly combed hair but for a few recalcitrant strands on the crown that constantly banded together to rebel. Our reunion began in silence, specifically the discretion imposed on the lovers by Cupid. But the sculptor's eighteenth-century masterpiece is also a reworking of the antecedent Harpocratic Eros whose iconic gesture of a finger lifted to his mouth is the mark of Horus in the ancient mystery cults. After nearly twenty minutes, Aristakes had yet to make a sound. There was nowhere to sit, and notwithstanding my appreciation for the objet d'art, I began to feel fidgety and awkward. My companion turned towards me looking vaguely annoyed.

"When I am gone, most of what you'll learn that is useful you will not hear from the mouth of people, but it will come from the heart of silence."

I felt a tinge of guilt rising, and I did not want to think about the implications of his words. Yet, my friend was never one to hold the same thought for long. With a smile, he relented.

"Let's go see the Salles Rouges." I did not realize then that, above all things, he wanted me to be free from pain and sadness, and he was determined to make the most of our time together in Paris. We shared the wealth of our youth, and I couldn't imagine it would run out so fast. One thing that did not dissipate though was Aristakes' apparently unlimited supply of money. I also learned the secret of his survival among the adults.

"To you, I am a reflection of your soul, to them, I appear in their image."

XII

We had our own way to discover the city. Aristakes had invented a "system" of random numbers we drew with the help of a spinning top that he insisted on calling a teetotum because it had markings on it much like dice. Once the "teetotum" had given us numbers, my companion would "interpret" them to determine in what direction and how far we would go by means of the Métropolitain. I've always wondered if there was anything to the game and if it was truly random, or if my friend was making things up to impress me. But it did not matter because we had so much fun. There is nothing in the world like the Parisian Métro, and nothing like Paris. I would go back many times over the years, but never again would it be the same without my bearer of light in the city of lights.

Each metro station that spat us out and back to the surface world would be our point of departure on a quest for oddities: an art nouveau facade, a commemorative plate, the birth home of a poet, the atelier of an artist, a tiny square with a single bench in the shade of a plane tree, an unappreciated fountain, or an unsung sculpture. We mapped the smaller museums and the quintessential Parisian parks that checked all the atmospheric tropes from the gaudy to the stately. We tarried in covered passages with art-deco *verrières* and quaint shops. We shunned the tourists, avoided the crowds, and played a few pranks at their expense. Aristakes told me that beauty and truth are generally shy creatures. They would rather avoid the attention of the masses, and yet we inflict them that burden, forcing them to endure the relentless glare of cameras until they lose their luster, not much different from the way we once exposed deviants to public abuse in a pillory.

We returned to the Louvre. My companion had asked me to wait for him at the Cour Carrée where the coq triumphs over the ouroboros in the east. I consulted Violette's 22-volume encyclopedia for "ouroboros" and "Cour Carrée," and I also picked her brain for useful information. Sure enough, from within the court one can see on the east wing pediment a rooster in relief perched on a serpent biting its tail. Aristakes showed up, visibly satisfied that I had solved another of his brain teasers. He took us straight to Hippolyte Moulin's *Secret d'en Haut* (do not look for the sculpture at the Louvre though, it has since been relocated to the newer Musée d'Orsay), and I understood the artworks he singled out served as headings in the imaginal book he was unfalteringly writing for me.

"Hermes is a liminal deity," he explained, "the messenger between the highest and the lower realms, between the gods and the mortals, and the guide of the human soul after death. Here, the youthful, celestial Hermes is whispering in the ear of his terrestrial and older counterpart in the form of the herma. Hermes learns from himself, and this is the secret he hears: *He who understands the beginning has found the end. Therefore he stands at the beginning and the end, knowing not death.*"

By then, I was used to Aristakes' obscure mystifications, but this latter one had crossed a new esoteric threshold beyond my grasp. Fortunately, relief was in sight in the form of another tale my companion was eager to share with me. I liked his stories, and especially the parts that he narrated as if he had lived them.

"There was once a very old king who reigned over a vast kingdom," began the storyteller. "So vast was his domain in fact that he himself knew not its boundaries. But the monarch wasn't always an absolute ruler. The story had its genesis in much earlier times when there was no story to be told because there was no human to hear them. There were the gods of course, but they do not listen to stories, they live them. Among the gods were Father Sky and Mother Earth. Unsurprisingly, those two were a couple, and the children they begat were the human race."

"I thought humanity came out of Dionysus' stone," I interjected unwisely. And Aristakes wasn't too happy I interrupted the flow of his story with such a jejune remark.

"All stories are true even if they contradict each other," he said a bit petulantly. "All stories are true," he repeated, "because they all tell us something about ourselves." And he carried on with his own.

"The children of Earth and Sky were unruly, quarrelsome, insolent, and demanding, which at first wasn't too much of a problem because they lived as sparse tribes over large regions. But unlike the gods they also multiplied like rabbits, and their parents had better things to do—like living new stories—than caring for the offsprings they never planned in the first place. Destroying all their children would have been unbecoming of a true god though, and so they conceived an alternative plan. They called upon one among the humans who was the most cunning of all, and his name was

Yaldabaoth. They made a pact with him whereby he would rule over humanity in exchange for immortality, prestige, immense wealth, and enormous power. The deal was sealed, and Yaldabaoth set off to work.

"The first order of the day was for him to give mankind dominion over the earth and the means to exploit its resources with maximum efficiency. Thus he implanted greed in the heart of man because a people motivated by greed is malleable in the hands of the crafty ruler.

"Next, Yaldabaoth contrived to undermine analytical thinking and doubt in favor of practical knowledge and skills, because the system requires workers and servitors but no philosopher to question the system."

Aristakes had found a rhythm for his story, and he told it as we slowly paced the galleries, occasionally taking an intermission over a fantastic objet d'art such as the dreamy *Les funérailles de l'Amour*.

"The common assumption is that you can control ideas and beliefs by withholding information. For example, you can ban books. But the likely result is that you will only make people curious about what you banned. On the other hand, if you have a hundred experts on the same matter who all contradict each other, things start working in your direction. So, Yaldabaoth saturated the masses with conflicting viewpoints so as to disorient and divide them. Reasonably intelligent people thought they were blessed with such a wealth of information and profusion of perspectives, but in truth, everybody grew amenable to confusion and swallowing lies. And the harder it was to separate the good seedlings from the weeds, the more popular sound bites and claims of absolute truths became.

"Notwithstanding his success, Yaldabaoth wasn't finished yet. He built a gigantic pyramid of oversight and regulations with himself at the top. Everyone in the structure had just one job to perform, and their reward was to take advantage of those underneath. But Yaldabaoth had yet to be satisfied.

"Immortality is a long stretch, and the humans had all but lost sight of who sat removed and isolated on top of the pyramid of control and the nebulous hierarchy of power. To remind everyone of his existence, Yaldabaoth had a set of rules inscribed on golden tablets, and he sent messengers throughout all the nations declaring: 'This is the law of Yaldabaoth your God, and there is no other god than him.

"As befitting a king who built himself into a god, Yaldabaoth had a personal guard of 360 elite warriors whose leader was no ordinary mortal either."

Aristakes fell silent for a few seconds in order to amplify the dramatic tension of the story.

"Humans and animals are not the only creatures dwelling on Earth. Among them also walk in concealment the elementals and the accidental gods. For instance, when the Moon god fell in love with a river nymph, they had a son whom they named Eosphorus because he was born at dawn. He was a well-favored, charismatic fellow who in time rose to become the captain of the king's personal guard. Eosphorus cared for the humans, and the humans loved him. He undertook to protect the meek and the defenseless when Yaldabaoth only told them to turn the other cheek. Everywhere he went he was celebrated for his wisdom, his generosity, and his fairness. Above all else, Eosphorus had elected to remain among the mortals because he desired to help them become gods like himself. From his father he knew that beyond the celestial spheres and the stars, there are splendid realms of beauty, harmony, and light of which mere humans could become the inheritors with the help of an unselfish god. Hence, he had entered the service of the king hoping that the suzerain would embrace his cause. Far from acceding to his vision though, Yaldabaoth became jealous of his captain who, unlike himself, was a true god, and because Eosphorus was so popular. So the son of the moon and the river nymph grew disheartened and discontented with the king who was increasingly vain, authoritarian, and callous.

"Now the self-proclaimed God Almighty craved the unconditional devotion and adulation of his subjects. And once more as the supreme ruler, he proved resourceful and came up with a brilliant ploy. *Surely*, thought Yaldabaoth, *if I could flaunt the fanatical faith of just one man willing to make the most shocking sacrifice for my sake, the people would revere me with awe.* And so, with a flair for grandstanding, he convinced an impressionable simpleton to stage the sacrifice of his own son in a way that would play well to the crowd. But when the time came and the simpleton was about to plunge a knife into the youthful flesh of his heir, Eosphorus intervened and stayed his hand to stop the horror. The king was furious, but not wanting to lose face, he claimed it was he who had sent the captain of his guard to restrain the overzealous worshipper. Yet, because Yaldabaoth loved the sight of spilled blood, the wails of agony, and the scent of burning flesh, he asked the simpleton to sacrifice him a ram instead. Eosphorus' intervention turned into a silver lining for the king that he himself had not anticipated: For millennia to come, the masses would praise the magnanimity of the God of Abraham alongside the unwavering faith of his servant who was willing to slay his own child.

"Thus had the rex mundi outsmarted Eosphorus, and he now turned his anger against the captain of his guard. Eosphorus for his part had turned one third of his men against the tyrant, and they all went into exile swearing to defeat the ruler's aims. Henceforth, they would covertly abide among the people of earth and impart to anyone with an ear to lend the esoteric know-how to free themselves from the shackles of the world of pain and suffering."

Aristakes looked at me with a half-hindered sly smile on his lips and continued:

"This could be an adequate conclusion to the story, but unfortunately for Eosphorus, the king had another splendid idea. He drew from the antecedent pagan mythologies and a good deal of imagination to create and circulate a new myth in which he recast his former right-hand man as a fallen angel who, because of his pride, was banished and repudiated by the one true God. Henceforth, the Light of Dawn, son of the moon and the river would be remembered in the memories of mankind as a dragon, or a cloven-footed devil with horns and a tail who reigns over the pit of hell where those who deviate from the law are sent to be tortured for all eternities. Because most people dreaded hell and feared the devil, they turned their heart even more fervently toward Yaldabaoth, their God whom they called the Heavenly Father.

"There are three races of humans, you see," explicated Aristakes, "and those have nothing to do with the color of their skin, the language they speak, or their area of origin. They are the *Terrestrial*, the *Celestial*, and the *Heirs of Dawn*. The first is bound to the earth: they see the door and do not bother to ask themselves where it may lead. The second is bound to the cosmos: they stand at the door fumbling with keys, wondering which one may work and trying them all. Now and then, they add a new key to their already heavy set. The third is boundless: they kick the door and let themselves in. Among the latter are found many poets, artists, children, and true dreamers who all have the imaginal capacity to see through the opaque veil of the stars; they are often called loners, misfits, deviants, and heretics. And because, logically, nothing is truly unimaginable, there is no greater power bestowed upon the human soul than that of the imagination.

"To replace his defunct guard, the king marshalled a new elite corps called *Domini Canis* to hunt down the heretics, that is anyone who disagreed with his rule and those who sided or sympathized with his former ally. The "Lord's hounds" were not the brightest, but they were the most fervid acolytes, which made them dreadfully efficient. In the end, very few individuals would listen to Eosphorus and his marginal band of rebels."

The story troubled me. Ever since I had crossed paths with him on the stairs of the school, I sensed Aristakes was skillfully weaving a web of words and images at the center of which he willed me to join him, and I clumsily got stuck on every strand. I had drawn conclusions of course, but they led me to questions I was afraid to answer.

"I think that's why I am more of a cat person," declared my companion wryly before bursting out laughing. We had walked into the gallery of Egyptian antiquities, and the goddess Bastet was peering at us from behind her window. She had amber eyes.

XIII

With so much to see and do in the City of Love, four hours a day was paltry, and Aristakes implored me to find a way to spend one entire day together. His tone of voice was one thing about him I had learned to read, and this latter request suggested another separation was approaching. I begged Emmanuel for more time on my own, but he was increasingly concerned my escapades would get him in trouble. Still, with an abundance of guarantees and an offer he could not refuse on top of that, I got a deal. We told his mom we would be heading to Versailles early on the morrow and visiting till late afternoon.

XIV

I arrived at the Place de la Bastille just after sunrise, unsurprised to see Aristakes already there standing by the Colonne de Juillet, which was our rendezvous point. He was drawing in his sketchbook as was his customary pastime. Though unfinished, the illustration appeared to portray a nude woman kneeling on the riverbank underneath an oversized five-pointed star up in the sky. I did not expect a comment on the drawing, and I didn't get any; I did expect a tangential observation, and there it was:

"I find it perplexing that so many people legitimately want freedom on Earth, and yet so few of them seek freedom from the earth." I guessed he was referring to the Genius of Liberty, stark naked with a star in his hair, airily perched on the tip of the monumental column. And I smiled indulgently because I still had to fully understand the implications of his allusion.

"That is why humans are made to believe they are masters of their fortunes. When they are credulously striving to create their own destiny, like distracted toddlers straining to assemble Lego bricks, they have no time to think of escaping the world of fate."

I was hungry, and my companion must have read my thoughts, which I suspected he was always able to do.

"We will eat first. We have so much to do." He was full of joy, and nothing could have made me happier. From the Bastille Square we took the metro to the Île de la Cité and found a café bar to relax and dunk croissants in our café au lait. After breakfast, we walked to our first destination and sat in the shade of the chestnut trees. The triangular Place Dauphine with its funnel-like ingress, bordered on two sides by residential buildings and at its base by the imposing Palais de Justice, was a peaceful retreat in the busy heart of Paris. Like an old bastion, it repelled the assaults of the populace and the fracas of tourism.

"You and me," said Aristakes, "we are the new heretics." He pulled out his pocketknife, and while I looked for interlopers, he carved on the seat of a wooden bench our very own commemorative epigram:

Il y a bien des années ici
Defiant la divine autocracie
Les hérétiques nouveaux étaient assis.

My companion was better at drawing than he was a poet, but *peu importe*! With the pocketknife we drew blood from the *vena amoris* of our ring fingers and smeared a couple of mixed drops on the trunk of a chestnut tree: the crimson mark of our bond.

Our breakfast and Aristakes' carving prowess had already scraped two hours off our schedule, and we hurried to our next stop, the Sainte-Chapelle nearby, worth visiting for its stunning array of stained-glass windows. On the other hand, we skipped Notre-Dame, which would have been worth exploring by a full moon at night when totally deserted (I was hoping Aristakes would take me to do just that) but was overrun by tourists during the day. After a brief tour of the Sainte-Chapelle, it was only fitting that we went to pay homage to the archetypal victim of a zealous religious establishment in cahoots with the greedy secular power. This we did a short distance away at the Square du Vert-Galant, standing on the spot where some seven centuries before, Jacques de Molay, the last of the Templar Grand Masters, was cruelly executed.

Aristakes gazed in silence at the commemorative plate as if reminiscing about events he had witnessed personally.

"De Molay and his companion Geoffroy de Charnay died very courageously after years of torture and rotting in prison," he said, breaking his observance. "The *Domini Canis* used to be more overtly violent. For centuries, the Spanish inquisition, formed predominantly of Dominican and Franciscan monks, hunted down Jews and heretics whom they subsequently had tortured, paraded in public, and burnt at the stake. They choreographed public spectacles in which their victims were humiliated and sadistically killed for the edification of a cheering populace and the gleeful satisfaction of clerics. They called those Christian abominations *auto-da-fé*, that is an 'act of faith.' Such practices might have disappeared, but the hounds are still among us. They have adapted to the changing times, and their methods have become more covert and psychological, though no less effective. They have considerably broadened their focus to encompass most aspects of society that help them keep control of mankind's perception. They are not bound by any creeds or religions and can use all beliefs and science to further the interests of their master the rex mundi."

It was to be our day together though, and we didn't want to dwell on so gloomy a thought. Unfortunately, people were already crowding the exiguous verdant urban space we would rather not share with anyone. We moved on.

The itinerary Aristakes had conceived would take us to the Bibliothèque Mazarine, the Palais Garnier, and the Tour Saint-Jacques. We had our lunch by the Fontaine Médicis, and we also spent time browsing the stalls of the Bouquinistes on the banks of the Seine or loitering in parks. We made the most of our time hardly feeling any fatigue, and by early evening we retired to the nearly deserted Square Barye. Not as much of a draw as its counterpart on the western end of the Île de la Cité, the narrow park on the eastern tip of the Île Saint-Louis with its exotic trees from around the world was more charming for being less popular. We took a rest in front of the Monument à Barye that displayed a pair of the artist's sculptures: *Force Protecting Work*, and the curiously named *Order Punishing Perversity*.

"*L'ordre et la force!* Might as well be the motto of the *Domini Canis*," remarked Aristakes sarcastically. We took the stairs down to the cobbled embankment, and I sat with my feet dangling over the steady run of the river. My friend lay on his back, his knees drawn up, his head on my lap. I gazed into the cool flame of his eyes, but his own sight was lost in the crown of the venerable trees towering above us. We stayed as long and late as we could.

XV

"It's only four days," my companion had reassured me just before we separated. He said he needed the time to finish working on his sketchbook; I couldn't see why I wasn't supposed to tag along. His request to be alone even for a short while unnerved me, and I acted like the capricious child though, at least in appearances, I was now older than he. It bothered me that he could so easily see through to my soul when I was constantly struggling to decipher his mind. What did he want? Why the recurring separations and reuniting? Why couldn't he make sure we would always be together? Yet, after a good night's sleep, I regretted my petty tantrum.

At least, the recess gave me the chance to fulfill my promise to Emmanuel, and the interlude that followed turned out to be very satisfying. My accomplice wasted no time in revealing to me all his secrets and immediately introduced me to his partners in crime. They were Timofey and Semyon, the two Russian exiles whom we called "the twins" although they were not related (but they were inseparable), and Eugène Sébastien Victoire, whom we called "Vic" for the obvious reason. Vic's mother was Moroccan, his father Guadeloupean, and I found his *Métis* mix especially intriguing. The little band was convivial, and I thought Aristakes would have liked them too. They were rebels in their own adolescent ways. Manu surprised me by being more cultured than I had assumed him to be. I made an attempt at sharing a selection of my own secrets with him, but he did not believe a word of it. He was very impressed with my imagination though.

The gang dragged me to smoky, boxy bars where I sipped cocktails of Pastis, grenadine, and Orangina while they held symposia about philosophy, politics, and current affairs. They were familiar with *décadentisme* and *existentialisme* and of course thought of themselves as way beyond their years. They listened endlessly to Pink Floyd's *A Saucerful of Secrets* and *The Dark Side of the Moon*. Timofey had an 8mm camera with which he recorded our antics, the highlight of which was our trip to the undisclosed location of an underground quarry.

Vic's parents were the caretakers of an eighteenth-century residential building, and like many in their trade, they occupied a modest apartment just below street level. Vic had befriended an older tenant who was a veteran of the two great wars and showed the stripling in confidence a hidden passageway underneath the property. It led to a succession of tunnels and chambers that had been used by insurgents in the tempestuous days of the Commune and, 70 years later, by the Parisian resistance during the German occupation. Less probable but no less thrilling, Vic swore that the place had also been the haunt of an occult society (I believe he had gotten that from a popular TV series though). At the heart of the underground network was the quarry that had been re-claimed as the exclusive headquarters of "les 4 au 5" as Manu, Vic, and the twins called themselves (a reference to the number of them, and the arrondissement where Vic's family resided). They had brought everything they could possibly carry down the cavernous chamber to make the place comfortable. We toasted our clandestine assembly with wine, and I was made

Lord of the Misrule for a day, wielder of the preceptor's staff. At last, I was initiated in the rites of the thiasus of four and made an honorary member of "les 4 au 5."

XVI

My four days away from Aristakes had panned out wonderfully, although at all times I found myself wishing he was with us. Now, at the completion of my Orphic journey, I was exhilarated to return to my light. *I will be where Zephyr and the moon linger together* was my companion's clue. I was supposed to follow the wind...

That was his signature play to lure me with its subtle mysteries, and I was elated when they surrendered to me. This once, the solution was easy because we had walked through the "Red Rooms" of the Louvre before where the painting of which Aristakes was so fond was prominently displayed. As expected, I found him in rapt attention of Anne-Louis Girodet's masterwork in the Salle Daru. He looked so composed and angelic in contrast to my rather rowdy friends of late. I did not want to disturb him out of his reverie. I sat next to him in the center of the room. He knew I was there, and that was enough to keep me content like a purring cat on the lap of his master. The gallery, with its parquet flooring, crimson walls, and glass ceiling diffusing the light over neoclassical paintings felt suspended in time. Unaffected by the changes of the outside world, it revealed to me its secret nature: an esoteric hub where I could learn from the canvases the initiates' wisdom long guarded by the sphinx, heard by Psyche from the lips of her lover, taught by Chiron to his pupil Achilles. Of all the paintings on the walls though, it was *Effet de Lune* that held Aristakes in a trance. Indeed, after staring at the art piece for a moment, I too imagined Zephyr and the moon leaping off the oil paint to play with me while Endymion and the dog were sleeping. Without shifting his gaze from the slumbering Aeolian ephebe, my friend spoke to me.

"I'll be watching you while you sleep, grow old, and forget." With his chin, he motioned toward the dog at the feet of Endymion. "They are guarding the door of the bridal chamber and let no one enter."

"When he was half-mad with despair, Goya painted on the wall of his home a series of disturbing, surreal images—his way of exorcizing the horrors of war, superstition, religious fanaticism, and decrepitude he had experienced in his lifetime. One of those paintings may be the greatest image ever produced by the human psyche—minimalist and yet unparalleled as an expression of the human condition: a dog trapped and about to be engulfed in matter looks up pitifully toward his unhelpful master in the shape of a looming, indistinct shade."

Aristakes turned his head toward me, and the forlornness in his eyes gripped my soul. I think he did not want to let me process his words immediately.

"I have a gift for you," he now said impromptu as if his previous thought had already ebbed away into the vast ocean of his mind while I was left ashore. My friend handed me his sketchbook. All his drawings had been inked and colored with pastels, and they were strikingly beautiful. I'd never thought he would give them to me, and my heart melted with the hues on the paper.

"I need some air," Aristakes then said oddly.

We left the museum, passed the Arc de Triomphe du Carrousel, and walked down the main axis of the Jardin des Tuileries. I had my hands in my pockets, and my friend locked his arm around mine. When we reached the Grand Bassin, he fetched two chairs, and we sat next to the statue *Le Serment de Spartacus*. I was holding the sketchbook on my lap, and Aristakes flipped through it, giving me pause to appreciate while he offered sparse comments on some of them (something he had never done before), pointing to details with his finger. Each drawing had a title written in calligraphy at the bottom.

"Those are the Tour de l'Inquisition and the Tour du Tréseau. They exist for real." (*La Lune*)

"This is you... And the little dog is not your friend." (*Le Vagabond*) He chuckled.

"This is us." (*Le Soleil*)

"The dead are not alive, and the living will not die." (*L'Épreuve*)

"This one (*Le Mystique*) I copied from a work called *Homère et son guide* by the painter William-

Adolphe Bouguereau—his best, as far as I am concerned. In time, its meaning will completely unfold for you.

"We were there..." (*La Maison Dieu*)

Once we had gone through all the pages, he concluded:

"This is our story; only you will be able to read it."

Presently, I remembered I had a gift for my friend as well. I pulled out of my pocket an alabaster rook I had purchased at the flea market for a fortune in terms of a tween's allowance budget. But I thought it was pretty and worth the expense. Though the crown of the tower was chipped, the details were finely carved, and it looked genuinely quite old.

"I have a present for you too," I said, embarrassed of not having something more impressive to offer. But he took my offering with his two hands as if it were the most precious object he had ever seen. He embraced me tightly, and it should have been perfect except that something felt terribly amiss, something like the moment in a dream when the dreamer realizes he is dreaming, just before awakening.

"My future that takes refuge in you will be your purity through life," he muttered. And these were his last words. And he let go of me.

XVII

The garden had turned unnatural, the atmosphere eerily oppressing. I became aware of people crowding us too close for comfort.

"We need to go," I said feeling agitated. I got up; it was a mistake. I got slightly dizzy and disoriented. Figures around us continued to multiply and wedged themselves between Aristakes and I, and all I could firmly hold into my awareness was the sight of his gray eyes fixed on me until his seraphic face was stolen by the mass of flesh that pushed and pressed, dragging me away. I shouted in anger, but no sound came out of my mouth, and with each surge of ire the crowd expanded. I struck at the shades with my fist, but my arms were limp and my blows weak and ineffectual. The throng of numb bodies had grown considerable, and my head throbbed. I was awfully nauseated and overtaken by a debilitating bout of vertigo (a symptom of Ménière's disease from which I suffered during my youth). Thankfully, I blacked out.

For half a minute after I recovered consciousness, I had no notion of who and where I was or how much time had elapsed. Memories are the most extraordinary mystery yet to be cracked by science or religion, an enigma not at the edge of the universe, but within us. Whither do they go when they vanish? Whence do they come when they suddenly reappear, seemingly re-assembling themselves from scratch to define once again who we are, our likes, our expectations and our fears, our desires and our beliefs?

Three persons were bent over me inquiring about my wellbeing. From the distance they had seen me falling and rushed to help. There were a few other onlookers, but it was the lady nearest me who insisted on giving me a lift home. She was exceedingly considerate and left me in the care of Violette after detailing to her the circumstances of the incident. Because of my weak state, I was mercifully spared the need to explain anything or answer questions, but Manu was in trouble. I was grateful he managed to extricate himself from the thorny situation. Picking up clues rapidly, he reported how we got separated when he went to the bathroom and I wandered outside the museum. He apologized profusely, insisting he had been looking for me all this time. It was plausible and convincing.

The next day, Violette took me to the doctor. Having no idea how to diagnose my symptoms, he blamed them on the onset of puberty. Still, out of an abundance of caution, and because of lingering doubts about Emmanuel's ability to watch over me, a decision was made to send me back to my own family the following day as the wisest course of action.

I would miss Manu and "les 4 au 5." I tried for a while to keep in touch with them, but each went his own way in life. A few years later, I learned that Manu tragically had died an untimely death while trekking in the Pyrénées mountains. For my part, I fell into a stupor, a sort of death of my own.

XVIII

The rest of the summer I spent in denial. Everywhere I went I expected to see Aristakes, and to facilitate that joyful expectation, I split most of my free time between libraries, bookstores, museums, public gardens, and old churches. But my amber stone would no longer glow.

Another school year began, and notwithstanding my contempt for the institution, at least it distracted me from my chagrin somewhat. Still, I found myself going back over again to the same spot where Aristakes had first made his presence known. I would stand in the hallway and spend the entire recess staring at the stairwell that once drew a seraph down from the heavens. My behavior unsettled the other kids, which had the advantage of keeping the bullies at bay but did not help my social life. I was able to make a few friends among the marginalized, but none could make me forget my aethereal companion. Could Achilles have forgotten Patroclus? Would David have replaced Jonathan?

Denial was taking me nowhere, and so I turned to supplication. I invoked all the gods who endeared themselves to me, begging, bargaining, promising, but no angel or daemon came to me as a bearer of good news. I even attempted to make the moon confess what it knew by capturing its reflection into a glass bowl filled with river water. But the moon and its reflection remained silent. With all my prayers unanswered, I retreated into quiet, resigned despair. My grades plummeted, and I had to repeat classes. I was now steadily growing toward manhood, and perhaps as a reaction to my loss, I yearned for it. I wished to be done with childhood as soon as possible, anticipating the changes and possibilities denied to the child but afforded by the adults.

I quit high school one year short of graduating to join the military. I had high hopes at first but was quickly disappointed with soldiering. Having enlisted as a minor, I was able to disentangle myself from contractual commitments after serving just one year (the length of the mandatory national service at the time). I went back to live with my family out of necessity, and I worked menial jobs befitting my lack of skills and education.

I nearly joined the Mormon sect, partly because I was infatuated with one of the missionaries who were so eager to teach me their "plan of salvation," and partly because I'd heard Joseph Smith was using a magical stone in his adolescent days. And I also found the pictures in *The Book of Mormon* pretty like those in fairy tale books. But the fetching missionary moved on, the story of the "seer stone" turned out to be a dead end, and the Mormon "Heavenly Father" looked to me like the spitting image of Yaldabaoth. Plus, I wasn't keen on such things as the laws of obedience and chastity.

I had now entered the kingdom of adulthood where, unlike in the realm of childhood, magic doesn't make any sense except for the loons. I began doubting my remembrance of the events that took place during my earlier years and found more reasons to do so as I lived through the decades of fantastical memories. Remembering "past lives" became a cliché. In a new trend, a substantial number of individuals distinctly recalled having been taken into alien spaceships then probed and poked with all sorts of low-tech instruments. That wasn't the end of it. Next, some poor souls were having vivid and lurid recollections (facilitated by charlatans) of childhood satanic rituals and sexual abuse that made for irrational headline fodder, creating a generalized panic and immense suffering. Down the lane, the amalgamation of occult superstitions led some people to swear they had witnessed famous entertainers and political figures shapeshifting into reptilian creatures and sacrificing children. Even without the intrusion of a paranormal dimension into our memories, there is still empirical evidence that we can never entirely trust what we think we remember. What in our lives is factual, and what is a story we keep telling ourselves sometimes with disastrous consequences? I put away in a box everything I had from Aristakes, wondering if I could have conceivably procured these items on my own.

With the money I received from a modest inheritance share following the death of my grandmother, I set off to the Pacific Islands, traveling on a budget, sharing with Aznavour and Gauguin the assumption that misery is more bearable under the sun. And speaking of the unconventional painter, it was in Tahiti that I had a chance to lay my eyes on his magistral work (on a loan from the fine arts museum of Boston) usually referred to by the three questions it literally raises: *Where do we come from? What are we? Where are we going?* And I reflected, *was the painting itself the very answer to the questions it raised, or were they both the product of Gauguin's own metaphysical angst?*

The following years (about four of them to be exact), I "island-hopped" from Tahiti to Bora-Bora, to Raiatea, Taha'a, Huahine, and back to Tahiti. To sustain myself, I work in the hospitality industry mostly, except in Taha'a where there was nothing and I relied on the generosity of the locals in exchange for odd jobs and tutoring the kids.

Before money ran out completely, I decided to travel to Hong Kong because I always wanted to see a slice of Asia. With my rudimentary English I was able to get by in the British territory, and I opted to stay there. I scraped a living by working as a Caucasian extra in a plethora of terrible Chinese movies along with the occasional spot on a TV commercial. I lived in Kowloon in a rental the size of an American bedroom, and I felt on top of the world because I had so little entanglement with it. I was freer than kings. I also made influential friends in the film industry who eventually procured for me a more lucrative opportunity that entailed constant travel between Asia and Europe. I loved it, and it gave me a chance to acquire the basics of other languages.

I saw the world. And the more of it I discovered, the more I saw a corpse—adorned with fineries, made-up to cover flaws, but a corpse nevertheless, a rotting carcass underneath the embellishments of mother nature. I heard the truth many times over, and each time it was different. I learned more about humans than through years of psychological studies, and the more I learned, the more I realized our nature is irredeemable, no matter the saintly acts we perform on rare occasions. And for those who still think it's a wonderful world, I have to ask, *why do we crave distractions so much if not to distract us from something we refuse to see?* I suspect the happiest people are those who manage to cram so many distractions into their lives that there is no longer room for disturbing thoughts. One thing I know because I lived through six decades of so-called progress: every promise that some aspects of our lives will be made easier is accompanied by a new level of complexity. And the more complex our existence, the less leisure we have to think about what it means to exist. Hunter-gatherers labored about twenty hours a week, and we have far less time off than even medieval peasants. Most of us work to enrich a handful of individuals who claim to hold the keys to our wellbeing and happiness. Meanwhile, what meager income we receive from the system we have in great part to return into the system just to afford necessities.

In my youth, I had been given the chance to begin feeling the marvels of a different world like someone brushing the contours of a fine statue before being stopped by an irate museum guard. But the realm that had appeared so possible once was now only faint echoes and furtive shades.

After a few years of being constantly on the move, it dawned on me that aging would soon put an end to my carefree lifestyle. Reluctantly, I made new plans once more facilitated by my Hong Kong connections. I settled in Canada, first to perfect my English, and then to resume my education that I managed to push into college. Yet, I could not decide on a major and lacked the drive to get into specialized studies. So, I looked for work again with two simple criteria: no job that would occupy my thoughts; nothing that could be misconstrued for a purpose. I found employment as a messenger, later as a security guard, and finally as a custodian in a private school, a position I still hold.

Thus could my existence have ebbed away and evaporated in the desert of life. And all regrets would have been moot because nothing could have been otherwise. I walk the path destiny has laid for me; excuses and justifications are irrelevant. We all strive to make the best decisions, but there is no guarantee they will be best and no telling what the consequences might be. Fate leads us, not a higher purpose. Fate and Death are the two companions that never for a moment leave us from the time of our birth to that of our exit. For some of us, there is a third.

XIX

At present, I live in Quebec. I rent a cozy apartment with a balcony that stretches near the crown of the trees in a quiet street. Not too long ago, an old crow took to visiting me almost every day, and I fed him crumbs from my meals. (After lengthy considerations I decided it was a male.) I felt for him. His plumage was dull and graying, missing in small patches around the neck. He was a solitary one, aloof from his kin, and he became my familiar. I'd never get tired of looking into the black depth of his eye that exuded a level of awareness our species still refuses to recognize in other earthlings. There was something else uncanny about my new companion (contemptuously ignored by the other, my cat Epimetheus) who became so confident as to perch on my lap and amuse me with his antics: with each visit, he brought along a piece of my memory that had flown away. The first time were lines by the poet Mallarmé that I had read when I was still a kid:

Il est une époque de l'Existence où nous nous retrouverons, sinon un lieu—et si vous en doutez le monde en sera témoin, en supposant que je vive assez vieux.

Subsequently, I baptized my bird "Anatole," after Mallarmé's deceased son for whom the poem was written.

Day after day then, I looked forward to the return of Anatole and the bit of memory he would carry. One morning, we were enjoying each other's company over breakfast when I found myself involuntarily lip-synching a word while hearing it echo in my mind: *Eosphorus*. Though I had not voiced the name, it had the effect of immobilizing my normally fidgety bird.

"Eosphorus," I now muttered on purpose. Anatole fixed me with one eye, and I was certain at that moment that his perception was attuned to my mind. And before I could recover from the moment of stupor, the crow had taken three hops and bolted in the air with a resonating caw. The next day, my winged friend did not show up, but I took that as a good sign. No longer was Anatole merely a clever corvid, I knew; he was a messenger between two lands. One of them no explorer of this world would ever spot on his physical horizons because it isn't affixed in space-time but afloat in apeiron. Now, these quivering shores were painstakingly reforming out of my shattered memories. And my words on the missive to the potentate of that expanse were: *I will remember*. And from then on, I would ceaselessly repeat in my mind the name of the one whom I loved most. I was confident this could take me into the heart of mystical silence, perhaps even to the spring of seraphic light. If not, I knew it would at least empower Aristakes wherever he might be.

On the twelfth day following my go-between's departure, the wind of Fate blew in an unsuspected direction. I was browsing a second-hand bookstore (a pastime that had stuck since my days with Aristakes) when I stumbled upon a used copy of *Contes Scandinaves*, the very same I had received from my uncle as a Christmas present back in the early 70s when nothing for me was more important than to carve a kingdom in the land of marvels. I came home with the volume under my arm and fell asleep at night with it still in my hands, open to the memorable illustration of Olaf's encounter with the king of the elves. In the morning I awoke with the urge to retrieve Aristakes' own drawings that he had created out of his love for me, and that I had put away because I could no longer bear to carry the memory of him with me. I stepped into my walking closet as I had done a thousand times before, and there was something distinctively different about the confined space lit by a weak yellow light. From a private alcove it had transformed into a Holy of Holies with its own Ark of the Covenant sitting in the corner of the top shelf, a plain box that for decades had harbored the secret of Aristakes' existence. I was angry at myself. How could the obvious have so easily escaped me. I had fallen into a self-inflicted dull somnolence, riveted by a delusion. In my disappointment, I had clung to the perception that I had been dragged away from

Aristakes, and that he had abandoned me. But what if he had been pulled away from me and I had abandoned him? Where would he be now? Where should I be searching? The answers, I told myself, were in that box. I did not rush to go through my friend's sketchbook though; I wanted to proceed slowly, with a clear mind free from undue emotions. I decided to strike a reverent pace proper to the complex task at hand. I put the sketchbook at my bedside almost ritualistically, as a sign it would be, from that moment on, the principal object of my attention. The amber gem I did put back immediately where it should have stayed all those years, hanging on my neck.

The following evening, I went to sleep clutching the pendant in my hand because it fascinated Epimetheus who kept trying to bite it. And once anew, the amber guided me, not through space, but through the treacherous world of dreams until I found myself in a place I had never visited before while in the embrace of the *Somnia*.

Unexpectedly, I was a pubescent youngster again, and I wore clothes from a forgotten epoch. I was standing in the midst of a glorious mountainous landscape with precipices, couloirs, and evergreens bathed in ethereal light and penumbra. I approached a fountain on the edge of which was sitting a dweller of the dream. I looked upon him, and his features were those of my long-lost comrade Emmanuel, only his countenance was nobler, and his allure immensely more striking like that of an archangel. I fell at his feet and wanted to worship him, but he took me by the hand saying that he who had sent him was greater than the messenger. He took me astride his horse who galloped away as if in midair, leaping from cliff to cliff with ease until we reached a peak and a cave that at first reminded me of the one I had visited with Aristakes in the mountains of Corsica. But when we stepped into its mouth, we stood before a monumental bronze double door. It was sculpted with representations of the three winged-boy gods, Thanatos, Hypnos, and Eros, who each lead the soul to a different sphere of perception through dying, dreaming, or longing. Thanatos figured on the left leaf, facing and beckoning the visitors. Hypnos graced the right leaf in profile with an index pointing to the flying Eros seen above and from the back, split between the two leaves. The doors were flung open, and we entered an immense nave with a vaulted ceiling under which glided a hierarchy of seraphim. The light in the nave came from their wings and was reflected by myriad pieces of colored glass and minuscule mirrors inlaid on the ceiling. The walls were adorned with decorated tiles and segmented by twelve stained-glass windows that were renditions of Aristakes' drawings. The seraphim whispered between themselves, and their conversation made an endearing sound not unlike that of the Italian poplars when the wind tousles their foliage.

At the far end of the nave, there was an altar, and beyond it steps led to a platform with an empty throne overlooking the sanctuary. Behind and above the throne hovered an intricate, massive rose window like a resplendent star that would aureole the sovereign and confer legitimacy to his empyreal rule.

Already, the implacable gravity of the waking world was pulling me back into its dreary morass, but before I tumbled out of the sphere of vibrancy, I heard an oracle resounding from the heart of the dream:

"The time is nigh, when a man wearied by the years will not hesitate to ask a child about the place of life, and that man will live."

XX

I woke up late for work. In a rush to get ready and catch a bus I couldn't reflect on the transmundane interlude of the past night, and before day's end, I had yet to be subjected to more troubling developments.

I worked my shift from 14:00 to 22:30 making an effort not to think too much. After securing the building I left the school and covered the short distance to the nearest bus stop, unaware of the peril rolling incrementally toward me. I waited at the crossroad light for my turn to step forward only to be startled by the glare of high beams and the roar of a speeding car. I had that couple seconds of hesitation not knowing whether to back off or move ahead, and the car closed in alarmingly, showing no sign of stopping. I leaped as fast and adroitly as my age would permit to avoid a frontal collision but got hit on the arm by the vehicle's right-side mirror. I was sent spinning, flopping, and slamming the pavement with my butt like a discomfited ballet dancer after a failed pirouette. As I saw it from the distance, the driver of the car had not fared better. After missing the sharp bend of the road, the overspeeding vehicle possessed by centrifugal force was sent crashing into a lamppost. It was good enough that other drivers were rushing to the scene, I wasn't going to get any nearer to that lunatic. In the dark, nobody had seen me. I trotted to the bus stop hoping my transport would arrive quickly.

Once safely at home, I was so shaken that I ate little, took a speed-shower, and hopped into bed. The following morning was Friday. I called in sick early and went back to sleep.

Two hours later, I was up and in a buoyant mood, physically and mentally unscathed by the fright of the previous night. While I was relaxing pensively over coffee and toasts, it occurred to me that, for the most part, childhood is as liberating as adulthood is manipulative. In fact, the two are so utterly distinct that we can speak of two separate realities, and not just in terms of biological or psychological factors. The perception of the child is a window opened onto a vast landscape with fluid boundaries, whereas grown-ups open their windows of perception to face a walled garden. It's no wonder the puberty years are so trying when one is forced bon gré, mal gré out of a budding paracosm and tossed into a deceptive reality. I decided to spend my weekend atoning for the years I neglected to give Aristakes' drawings the attention they deserved. A plan had already formed in my head. I had seen the cliché often enough in movies and TV series: an assiduous detective pinning photographs, newspaper clips, and sticky notes on a board and linking them with strings until a big picture could emerge before his eyes. The big picture is what I wanted, and I was at long last ready to do what it takes to see the story through to its end. I had all the pieces of the puzzle: Aristakes' drawings and my own memories. The drawings were far too precious to pin carelessly, but I could use frameless acrylic displays to hang them on the wall of my bedroom. They would be the first things I saw upon awakening, and the last before falling asleep. Presently, I carefully detached each piece from the spine of the sketchbook and spread them on my bed in the same order they were presented to me by my friend: *La Lune; Le Vagabond; Le Dupeur; Le Libérateur; La Révélation; L'Hérétique; Le Soleil; L'Épreuve; Le Mystique; La Pureté; La Destinée; La Maison Dieu; L'Étoile; Les Amants.* This was our story, and I had to decipher its poetry. My other task would be to recall every moment I spent with Aristakes. Every detail mattered because everything my friend did was intentional. He had left me a trail to follow; he was my grail at the end of the quest.

Our story began with the moon and would end with the lovers. But Aristakes had also said that the beginning was the same as the end. The lovers are where the heavenly moon is, and the moon-god was Eosphorus' father. Eosphorus is the harbinger of dawn, the morning star whose twin is Hesperus, the evening star—the beginning and the end, distinct but inseparable.

XXI

I spent months working on associations, analyzing every aspect of Aristakes' drawings. Nearly all my time was devoted to tearing the veil that concealed him from me. At work, while mopping floors and wiping tables, all my thoughts were directed at solving the mystery of his disappearance. In the age of the Internet, my effort was greatly facilitated with online searches, but I also followed many promising trails to dead ends and wasted too many hours in distracting back alleys. I lingered inquisitively at my local library, scanning rows of bookshelves to find pertinent publications and relevant information. From the bookstores I purchased thrice the number of volumes I already owned. I learned that the ancient Egyptians believed our essential nature to be dyadic. We have a *Ba* and a *Ka*, Soul and Essence, who could be reunited in the underworld, but only the chosen would become an *Akh*, a new star in the firmament, a god among the gods. The Manichaeans saw their essence as parcels of light that could be freed from the darkness of this world by a liberator and wheeled by the moon into the greater light of a living sun. Star, moon, sun, all figured prominently in the drawings.

I found out that a painting by the fascinating, yet perpetually misunderstood Hieronymus Bosch was likely the inspiration for Aristakes' "vagabond." Bosch's own tramp is an older man, wearied by the years, resolutely making his way back home after years of misery and solitude in the world. A vicious little dog threatens to attack the wanderer from behind, perhaps to send him in the wrong direction. It reminded me of the day I trekked to a small, quaint temple on the shore of Hong Kong. My excursion would have panned out smoothly if not for two nasty short-legged dogs no bigger than tabby cats, bent on cutting off the only path to reach my destination. They were so aggressive that I did not dare advance or turn my back to them, and nothing I tried would make them relent. At last, I was rescued by a kind villager who managed to chase the beasts away (either he knew how, or they knew him).

Nothing could deter our wayfarer though, because we meet him again seemingly farther on the way on yet another work by the Dutch master. He is not the sole unassuming creature to wander from one panel to the next. I first noticed the pygmy owl when it was perched on a branch above the traveler's path as if to spur him with encouragement. So, I followed the wayfarer, the owl, and even the dog to the so-called *Haywain Triptych* where they all reappear. Our traveler is still walking with the fiendish little dog hard on his heels while the unobtrusive owl has alighted on another branch at the top edge of the panel. At the bottom stretches the cortege of mankind and its rulers advancing inexorably toward their doom in the form of a tower still under construction. On the threshold, they are escorted into the edifice by grotesque demons.

While the blind are leading the blind to their grim fate, the bird of the night sees through the darkness of this world. I played a game of finding where the fifteenth-century owl could lead me next, and it did not disappoint. I had to look very carefully, but it is nearly always there in Bosch's paintings, unsuspected, often lurching in tight hideouts. It looks composed, sagacious, and endearing among the throngs of deformed creatures, demonic figures, and misshapen humans that crowd the artist's vision.

In *The Conjurer*, Hieronymus' owl is peeking from the inside of a tiny basket hanging on the belt of a street performer. It's witnessing the deception of the mountebank who captivates an unsuspecting crowd with sleights of hand while an accomplice steals their purses. Yet, a child among the onlookers is not distracted by the show and sees clearly what is happening. Such is the state of the world in which we live. Our attention is continuously misdirected and redirected with tricks toward worthless ends while what is of true value is stolen from us. Only children can see through the deception when they are not monitored and coached themselves. In the painting the little dog is still there, looking decidedly but deceptively tamed in his Fool disguise, for he is also watching carefully.

On the *Hermit Saints Triptych* my latest winged friend shows up twice, perhaps to bring my attention to a column of ascent in which a praying figure defies gravity and rises through the empyrean vault toward the spiritual moon and sun.

Everywhere it went through Hieronymus' oeuvre, the unprepossessed owl showed me things that I imagined Aristakes would have wanted me to see. But the last painting to which it guided me proved pivotal in my investigation.

XXII

Before I bade farewell to Hieronymus' owl, it invited me to be an invisible guest at a wedding feast, possibly the most anomalous scene painted by Bosch or, more likely, someone in his circle. My ghostly friend, of course, made itself inconspicuous on top of a cornice and behind a pillar from where it surveys a surprisingly serene assembly, far removed from the chaos and horror it had previously contemplated. The *Marriage Feast at Cana* is by and large unappreciated because of the incertitude over its origins, and because it lacks the lurid details and weird eroticism that makes Bosch's art so popular with the masses. It could be a very conventional religious tableau if not for the fact that it is ostentatiously and intentionally not looking anything like what it is supposed to represent. Here, the abundance of riddles makes up for the paucity of surrealist elements. The painting is based on a myth taken from the Gospel of John, but the artist has relegated the main actors of the story to the side as mere extras and put front and center a red-haired child who unconventionally turns his back to the viewer. Two little dogs in the foreground are eating crumbs fallen from the table of the master, but they cannot disturb the solemn, hallowed ceremony uniting the spirit-groom to the soul-bride. Richly dressed in his brocaded robe and white sash, the faceless child stands next to his throne. Wearing a crown on his head and raising a gold cup in his hand, he officiates in his princely and sacerdotal functions at the wedding of the lovers. Eosphorus the prince, Aristakes the hierophant, the child with many faces, the harbinger of light.

This wasn't exactly an epiphany; I had known intuitively that Aristakes and Eosphorus were one. But when I became a man, I put away "childish things," thinking they were the product of an unbridled imagination. In truth, I had abandoned my loving companion in time, in my childhood. That is where he was still, and where I would find him again.

I gave myself the task of meticulously gathering my memories, the result of which is the book you are reading. That in itself wasn't enough. I could not bring back Aristakes; I had to go back to him. But I was still missing the key that would allow me to bend time to my will. So I turned again to the drawings, examining them in reverse order.

The Lovers: The two squires face each other and exchange gifts: a blue stone for one, and for the other a shining pearl in a gaping clam shell. I had noticed the recurring symbol of the pearl in Bosch's paintings, but what did it mean? What was its relation to the stone of Dionysus? A large blank space had been left between the two standing figures—the only incomplete drawing...

The Star: The Zoroastrian priests had been led to the child-king by a star. It was the symbolic leitmotiv that accompanied Aristakes everywhere in my memories. Would it point to the direction I needed to follow?

The House of God: The dwelling of the god may be a church, but to the ancient Gnostics it was likely the temple-prison of flesh and bones in which the sovereign essence is trapped. Aristakes had drawn the main tower of the Cathedral of Strasbourg on fire with a collapsing spire, and the two dwarfed figures of the lovers escaping unscathed through the portal. On closer examination though (and with the benefit of the added coloring), the tower appears not so much engulfed in flames as consumed by an interior blaze.

Destiny: This one shows an oversized medieval-looking wheel of fortune with two kings clinging precariously on each side with arms and legs. Counterclockwise, one is rising, the other plummeting. At the top seats a little sphinx like an enigma. Was that the key? There was indeed a wheel in the Cathedral of Strasbourg, and Aristakes had taken me to it. It was the massive wheel window of the west portal.

The destiny of the lovers then was through the house of God. This was the connection; this was how the story ought to end. And the wheel held the key.

I had a high-resolution picture of the Strasbourg cathedral's wheel window set as a background on my desktop because it is so colorful and inspiring. *The secret of the wheel lies on its hub*, Aristakes had said. I fetched some tracing paper and applied it to the computer screen. With the stroke of a red felt pen I traced five lines connecting the five pieces of red glass in the center. At long last I had found the key, and I was overwhelmed with emotion.

XXIII

As soon as my request for time off was approved, I booked a trip to Strasbourg. Twice in my life I walked through the portal of the city's cathedral, first as a child, and half a century later as a man wearied by the years. Each time I had with me the amber stone Aristakes had given me. And again, I stepped into the dimness to find my light. When I reached the grand organ, I turned around, and from the center of the nave I faced west where the wheel of my destiny lay. The humongous eye fixed me benevolently, and I peered into its pupil with renewed childlike awe. I clutched the amber gem and whispered the sacred name.

There was a moment in timelessness, and nothing existed but I and the rose window before me: the rose of dawn. I penetrated its soft center; I let myself fall and be engulfed in the voluptuousness of its whorl. My awareness returned to a most primal state as I bathed in a palpable, comforting amniotic obscurity. Then, I emerged, 50 years younger, naked.

I was now facing the same stained-glass window but on the other side of the liminal wall that separates and adjoins the two sanctuaries in their respective dimensions. In Eosphorus' cathedral, seraphim were no longer fluttering under the ceiling, and the silence was absolute. The shimmer that filled the edifice, crisp and pastel as dawn, now emanated from the far end of the nave, from the elevated platform where the harbinger of light, the Levantine king, sat in splendor on his throne. He was more grown up now than I'd ever seen him, with hair the color of flames and eyes the color of amber. And I heard his voice still melodious and pure like the gentle flow of the creek:

"At last you are seeing beyond the veil. You cannot regain that which you have never lost, but you can always remember that which you have forgotten. You are the stone of Dionysus; you are one and many. The greatest lie ever wrought upon my children is that they are a thought in a higher consciousness. In truth, you are the consciousness, and there is nothing above. And when I have gathered all the heirs, the memories of mankind will abide eternally in me. I am the Son of Dawn, and you are my chosen. I am the beginning, and you are the twilight. The seraphic essence and the soul will be united forevermore; time is conquered."

I felt a swift, burning sting where the amber pendant touched my skin, and I awoke again in the existence we call reality. I heard a soft tapping on my window: Anatole had returned.

XXIV

That morning, bemused neighbors would see me holding a queer symposium over breakfast on my balcony with a cat and an old crow. Aristakes was there too, though no one but me could see him. He was always there, always with me in this world that we share but was never ours. I only had to look with the sight of eternal youth, which is the imaginal power that gives rise to ethereality. And should I ever begin to doubt or forget again, I need only feel with my fingertips the small scar burnt in the flesh next to my heart: the mark of Eosphorus in the shape of a star.

Printed in Great Britain
by Amazon